MEGA FREAK

BLOODY PARADISE

MIKE MACLEAN

SEVEREDPRESS

MEGA FREAK: BLOODY PARADISE

Copyright © 2025 By Mike MacLean

WWW.SEVEREDPRESS.COM

ISBN: 978-1-923165-58-8

ONE

In the darkness, Tino's eager fingers fumbled to unhook Mahana's bra. He'd been at it three entire minutes (it felt like ten) and he only managed to undo the top clasp. His tingly little neck kisses had stopped cold after the 90 second mark. Now he muttered under his breath in frustration.

"Come on. Come on."

Mahana reached back to undo the bra herself. "Don't worry about it, baby."

"It's this damn clasp. Who makes a clasp like this?"

"It's a Victoria's Secret. I got it on sale on Amazon." That was a lie. The bra was actually cheap knockoff brand—a *Miranda's Mystery*. But Tino didn't need to know that.

"It's a cruel joke," he said. "These bra makers must hate dudes or something. I bet they had themselves a good laugh making clasps like that."

"I'll do it, Tino. It's no big thing, really."

"No. I got it. I can't let it beat me."

Mahana could smell his flop sweat, seeping through a thick cloud of Axe body spray. His bra clasp ineptitude surprised her. Tino was a surf instructor after all, and those dudes were notorious man whores. From what Mahana heard, he and his six-pack abs had slept with half the resort staff and a high percentage of cougar tourists looking for some island boy action. But to be fair, the only light Tino had to work with were moonbeams shining through the window blinds. Mahana had left the lamps off in the bungalow so they wouldn't get caught by security.

The luxury bungalow was for VIP guests only. A thousand American dollars a night to stay in a place on stilts above a lagoon created by the island's vertical reefs. Gentle waves lapped against the support posts and a salty breeze swept in through the window. It was nice. But not $1000-bucks-a-night nice.

Of course, Mahana wasn't supposed to be in here, not unless she was mopping, scrubbing, and leaving origami towel swans on the pillows. She guessed sneaking in with Tino was part of the thrill of it. She had to admit, breaking the rules with the bad surfer boy was all kinds of hot.

But that was wearing off real quick.

Mahana bit her lip and let out a soft moan to encourage Tino to keep at it. Finally, he freed the last clasp. The bra slipped to the hardwood floor, landing on her rumpled maid's uniform.

Tino pumped a fist in the air. "Victory!"

Yeah, the heat was definitely wearing off. *What am I doing with this idiot?*

"Maybe this was a mistake," she said.

"No. We're good, baby." His soft lips brushed her earlobe as he whispered. "We're all good."

"But if we get caught… I just don't want to lose my job."

"Not gonna happen. I promise."

Then he began kissing her shoulder again, working his way up to her neck as his hands slid up to her breasts. And Mahana suddenly forgot all about her shitty cleaning lady job.

Oh, that's nice.

A rush of heat surged through her body. Tino's rough hand slipped to the curve of her hip. Slowly, he slid her panties down. Mahana's heart missed a few beats.

God, it'd been so long. What was it—two years without a man? That was unacceptable. She was way too hot to be manless for two friggin' years. Mahana needed this. She deserved this.

She grabbed the waistband of Tino's boardshorts and yanked them down with one quick jerk.

"Whoa! That's… Okay, let's do this…"

"Shhhh. Don't speak." Mahana kissed him hard, more to shut him up than anything else. He kissed her back, squeezing her ass. They shuffled clumsily towards the bed, their lips barely breaking contact.

This is happening. It's really happening.

Then Tino stopped kissing. Stopped squeezing. Stopped everything. In the moonlight Mahana could just make out his confused, furrowed brow.

"What? Why did you stop?"

"Did you hear that?"

Mahana gripped the back of his head and pulled him down towards her. "I didn't hear anything."

Tino shrugged and kissed her again. Frantic, Mahana spun him around and shoved him down on the bed. Then she climbed on top of him, giving him the "fuck-me" eyes and pouty lip combo, before realizing he probably couldn't see her face too clearly in the dark.

"Damn girl. You…"

There was a scratch at the bungalow door.

Tino squirmed out from under her and got to his feet. "You had to hear it that time."

Yeah, Mahana heard it. And she didn't fucking like it. Her heart began racing again, this time for a completely different reason. Without thinking, she grabbed handfuls of the bedspread and rolled her naked body up like a burrito.

"What was that?" she said.

Again, something scratched at the door. A faint sound, like a whisper in the dark.

Tino found a little towel on the pillow, one Mahana had folded into an origami swan for the apathetic resort guests. He wrapped the towel around his waist and stepped towards the door.

"Don't you open that door." There was more ice in Mahana's voice than fear. "You don't know what's out there."

"Ain't no predators on this island. One of the staff probably stowed a cat aboard the last boat."

"Fine. It's a cat. Leave it outside where it belongs and come back to bed."

Tino froze for a moment, like the decision-making process had hit the pause button on his brain. "It's distracting," he said finally. "If it keeps scratching like that, I don't know if I can…you know….."

"I heard you fucked Kika in the walk-in freezer while the kitchen staff prepared lunch."

Another scratch.

"I've gotta know." Tino grabbed the door knob. His lean muscles tensed as he crouched down, ready to spring into action. "Here kitty, kitty, kitty," he said. Then he flung the door open.

SQUEEEEEEE!

A blur of hairy flesh scrabbled across the bungalow's hardwood floors. It ping-ponged from wall to wall, emitting a high-pitched inhuman scream. Mahana cringed.

"Holy Hell! What is that thing?"

Tino flipped the wall switch, bathing the room in harsh light. Mahana squinted against it, searching the bungalow for their squealing invader.

"That is *not* a fucking cat," she said.

A wild piglet scampered under the bed frame—a runt, no more than a few months old. Its little hooved feet scratched the hardwood as it tried to burrow itself into the wall.

"Aww," said Tino. "The poor thing's terrified."

"Did you actually just say *aww*? What're you, a twelve-year-old girl?"

Stooping over, Tino held on to the towel wrapped around his waist and reached under the bed. "Hey there, buddy. No one's going to hurt you. Jesus, he's crazy trembling. Wonder what got it spooked?"

"That's a wild animal, Tino. It's probably all covered in lice, and fleas, and God knows what else. And now you're hugging it."

Tino had pulled the squealing piglet out from under the bed and squeezed it tight against his bare chest. The thing smelled like petrified poop shoved into a clammy running shoe. All the Axe body spray in the world wouldn't cover that up.

"Have you ever seen anything so cute?" Mahana sighed.

So much for her carnal desires. Tino was so busy soothing little Mr. Porkchops there, he'd forgotten all about Mahana's naked and willing body wrapped under the sheets. That was more than Mahana's pride could take.

She picked herself up from the bed and plucked her maid's outfit off the floor. She didn't bother slipping into her panties or bra. Instead, she jammed them into her purse and slid into her bland, gray dress. Its starched fabric rubbed against Mahana's flesh.

Tino watched the whole procedure while he snuggled and stroked his new best friend. At least the thing had stopped squealing its head off. Now the piglet just grunted and shivered.

"What're you doing?"

"Goodnight, Tino."

"You're leaving? But I thought we were having a nice time?"

Mahana didn't look at him or his pig. She stormed through the bungalow, searching for her flip-flops. "I'm not into threesomes."

"Ewww. I can't believe you said that."

"Wow. Are you actually covering the piglet's ears so it can't hear me?"

"No," said Tino, sliding his hand off the pig's ears.

"I hope you two are very happy together."

Mahana marched out the door, head held high. It would've been much more dramatic if it wasn't for the *clip-clop* of her flops against the boardwalk. She stalked past a few other identical bungalows until she ran out of deck and had to trudge up the beach. Her flip-flops sunk into the wet sand, leaving deep, angry footprints.

Up the hill, Tino's old Vespa scooter waited for her, resting against a crooked palm tree.

"Yo, wait up, girl!" Tino's bare feet slapped the deck boards as he jogged a dozen yards behind her. He hadn't bothered putting on his shorts and still gripped the towel tight to his waist. One slip and Tino's bare ass would be gleaming in the moonlight. His other hand clutched the piglet which had decided to start squealing its brains out again.

Mahana quickened her step. She knew Tino had left the keys in the Vespa's ignition, and she planned to use them. Why should *she* have to slog her ass all the way back to the employees' quarters. Let the pig-lover walk.

"Mahana, I…"

Tino cut off his own sentence so abruptly Mahana couldn't help but peek back at him. He wasn't jogging anymore. Just standing there at the edge of the boardwalk, gazing out at the dark shore. The pig squirmed like crazy, letting out one sharp "squeeee" after another. Finally, it struggled out of the surfer's grasp and hightailed it back towards the bungalows as fast as its little legs would carry it. Tino didn't even glance in the pig's direction.

"Tino, what's going on?"

"Don't you hear it?"

"What are you talking about?"

Before Tino could answer, a strange noise rippled across the beach. It was a hiss, for lack of a better word. Something about the sound of it reminded Mahana of watching her grandfather waste away in a hospital bed. His last breaths were angry, rattling gasps. She remembered thinking those breaths weren't human.

Mahana could no longer hear the gentle lapping waves or the rustling ocean wind. She could only hear the hiss, and it filled her with a dread she could not name. Maybe her ancestors had known that feeling well. But to Mahana—who dwelled in a world of condos and convenience stores—it was an alien fear. Something primal and long forgotten.

"I think we should go back to the bungalow."

Tino didn't budge an inch. "Where's it coming from?"

"Don't know and don't care. I just don't want to be here anymore."

The rattling hiss faded, becoming a soft whisper before dying down altogether. Tino stood still in the moonlight, scanning the beach. Then his shoulders slumped and he offered a nervous smile. "So weird. I wonder what it was."

An explosion erupted under Tino's feet. Something burst out from beneath the ground, sending a geyser of sand high into the air. A moment later, the sand rained down on a huge, insectile nightmare. The monster snatched Tino up with savage claws and bit his head off with terrifying efficiency. Blood sprayed from his severed neck.

Holy, fucking, shit.

Mahana knew she shouldn't scream. She knew doing so would only draw the creature's attention to herself. But she couldn't help it. One look at Tino's headless corpse and an ear-splitting shriek forced its way up her throat. She clamped one desperate hand over her mouth, but it was too late.

The thing turned its monstrous head in Mahana's direction and gazed at her with black, merciless eyes. Mahana screamed again. It was the last sound she would ever make.

TWO

Max leaned against the yacht's starboard rail, sipping a Hinano lager in the sunshine while seriously considering homicide.

They were in French Polynesian waters, sailing for Paradise Island, home to a world-famous resort for singles. The resort's pamphlet showed glossy images of pristine beaches, charming waterfalls, and of course beautiful bikini-clad women. Max wasn't exactly into the whole mingling singles thing. But the trip was free, so he figured he'd soak up some sun while sipping umbrella drinks.

Then he met this asshole and thoughts of murder danced in his head.

Max's intended victim was tall and lean with slick black hair and impossibly white teeth. The dude's vacation look was on brand—Bermuda shorts and a $300 Tommy Bahama shirt, unbuttoned to show off gold chains and bronze, tanning-booth skin. He leaned on the rail next to Max, filming himself—phone in one hand, vape pen in the other. He was, without question, a douchebag.

"Your boy Brody is on a boat, motherfuckers!" The douche—who was apparently named Brody— mugged for the camera as he spat out a stream of strawberry flavored vape smoke. "We left Tahiti about two hours ago, sailing to Paradise-fucking-

Island. You know what that means, boys. Hunting season's about to begin. And I got my sights on some prime tail."

One little push, Max thought. *I'll claim it was an accident.*

The douchebag nudged Max with his elbow and aimed his phone at him. Max didn't get seasick, thanks to his years in the U.S. Marine Corps. But right now, on the deck of this particular boat, sailing on calm waters, he wanted to puke his guts out. It was probably the gallon of cologne the douchebag wore, mixing with that vape pen smoke.

"What's up, fellow bro?" the dude asked. "You ready to get crazy?"

"No, thank you," Max said flatly. He took a sip of his beer and kept his eyes on the ocean.

"What do you mean *no thank you*?"

"I'm not interested in being on your podcast or whatever it is."

The douchebag made a lemon-sucking face. "Ain't no podcast, bud, It's a YouTube show. *The Blockchain Bro.*"

"And I'm sure it's great."

"Fuck yeah it is. Got two hundred K followers, bud. I sling get-rich, crypto advice. Throw in some luxury lifestyle vids. Viewers eat my shit up like it's French vanilla, know what I'm saying?"

"Nope, and I don't care. Just want to drink my beer and look at the water."

"Bullshit. You gotta know who I am."

Now, Max looked at him. "Yeah. You're the guy who's about to have a phone shoved up his ass.

Now stop fucking filming me, please and thank you."

The dude gave Max a dose of stink eye, but lowered his phone. "It's a public space. I've got the right to film whoever I want."

"Go film whoever you want somewhere else."

The yacht swayed as it rode the crest of a wave, causing the douchebag to stagger as he walked away. "You're lucky I wasn't live. Would've ruined the whole damn stream."

Max shook his head and turned his attention to the sea again. Back on the dock in Papeete, he noticed the guy as they boarded the yacht. Max guessed he was in his early thirties, financially comfortable and, like the rest of the guests, American. There were maybe sixty singles in all—some middle-management bros, a couple of trust-fund yoga princesses, and a pack of corporate boss bitches letting their hair down. They were all bright, beautiful, and ambitious.

Max felt like a complete outsider.

He grew up in a blue-collar family which struggled to make ends meet. He had a decent brain in his skull, but not decent enough to earn a scholarship. So he joined the military to escape the threat of poverty and picked the Marine Corps to challenge himself. The Marines gave him stability and purpose. But after a few tours of humping the desert and getting shot at, Max had enough.

He was tending bar and bouncing in a dive college club when he met Sharron. Two months later, they were shacked up and talking about *their* future. She'd get her real-estate license, and he'd attend business classes at the community college while doing double shifts on the weekends. They didn't have much money, but they laughed a lot and ripped off each other's clothes whenever possible. For the first time in his life, Max realized what happiness felt like. And he had a purpose again—to build a life with this woman.

Then Sharron met another guy.

One of the yacht's crew turned up the volume on the boat's sound system, intruding on Max's memories. A too-happy voice blared from speakers backed by a festive island tune.

"*Bonjour,* singles! This is your captain speaking." His flawless English was seasoned with a generous dash of Polynesian French. "We will be docking in Paradise Island's beautifully scenic north bay in thirty minutes. Until then, enjoy the tunes, sip your cocktails, and get ready for the adventure of a lifetime."

A chorus of cheers and half-drunken *woo-hoos* erupted from the singles.

Max drained the last of his beer and moved to the bow of the yacht so he could get a look at the island. On the horizon, the sun dipped low, painting the water gold and making a halo for the little island they approached.

It was such an amazing, postcard-perfect sight, Max forgot the douchebag and feeling like an outsider among the beautiful singles. He even forgot about Sharron for the first time in months.

Maybe this trip wouldn't be so bad.

THREE

"Noooooooooo!"

Rebecca had kicked too hard. Now she watched her brand-new soccer ball take two wild hops before bounding right into the jungle.

Ah shit.

Rebecca wasn't allowed to say the S-word out loud. But Mom couldn't stop her from thinking it. Her soccer ball rolled to a stop under the shady trees, plunking halfway into a thick bush. Which really sucked because Rebecca wasn't allowed to go into the jungle alone—another one of Mom's rules.

"Stay in the clearing," Mom had said, her face going all frowny. And she made Rebecca repeat it, like Rebecca was still some dumb little kid instead of a big nine-year-old.

The clearing wasn't anywhere near the big fancy house or the resort hotel. Now that the guests were arriving, Rebecca wasn't allowed to play by the hotel anymore. Which was bad because there were no swimming pools out here. Just a bunch of dirt and chopped up trees surrounding a giant hole in the ground. Bulldozers and other construction trucks sat there all quiet under the sun. They were gonna build a *new* hotel out here—a "north wing of the resort" her mom had called it. Mom was a geologist. It was her job to make sure the land was okay to make a building on. That was super boring if you asked Rebecca. She wished her mom could be a pro soccer player instead. Then Rebecca could go to her games and cheer her on from the stands.

Who wants to cheer for a friggin' geologist? Rebecca thought. *Nobody, that's who.*

Slowly, Rebecca stepped towards the edge of the jungle. She squinted her eyes. It sure was dark in there, all the leafy trees blocking out the golden sunset. Kinda spooky. But Rebecca could still make out her ball, wedged into the bush.

It's right there.

Rebecca looked over her shoulder at the trailer. It wasn't too far away. Maybe the length of a soccer field? They'd set it up near the big hole, close but not too close. Inside the trailer was the office where Mom worked on the computer. Outside was one of those generator things that made electricity. It made a loud humming noise.

Right there. The ball was right there. Mom wouldn't care if Rebecca went in and got it. Especially if she never found out.

Rebecca stepped all sneaky-like into the shadows of the trees. She wore pink Nike running shoes with matching shorts that her mom bought in Honolulu. The ground felt soft under the Nike's heels, kinda mushy. And bushes scratched at her bare legs. Every five steps or so, she glanced over her shoulder at the trailer again, making sure Mom hadn't come out.

Rebecca *knew* she was doing something naughty and her heart sped up. It wasn't such a bad feeling. Rebecca grinned.

Almost there.

Sweat rolled down Rebecca's forehead. It felt like the air was wet. It got darker and darker with every few steps. She sure hoped she wouldn't see a creepy jungle bug, maybe feel it skitter up her leg. But she didn't see any bugs. She didn't hear any either. The whole jungle went all quiet. Rebecca could hear the trailer's generator humming. But now it seemed far away.

Rebecca finally reached the ball and tugged it out of the bushes. She turned to run back to the clearing, back to the sunlight. That's when she heard it.

Hisssssssssssss.

Rebecca froze. She felt like she was suddenly stuck in cement and couldn't move. Her heart sped up again. This time, Rebecca didn't like how it felt.

The shady jungle got even darker. Like something was behind her. Something big enough to block out the sunlight. And Rebecca sensed something behind her too—like that weird feeling you get when you *know* someone has walked into a room, but you haven't seen them yet.

The hissing sound got louder. Slowly, Rebecca began to turn her head.

"Rebecca! Dinner time."

The sudden shout almost made Rebecca jump right out of her sneakers. It was her mom calling for her.

"Rebecca, what are you…" Mom didn't finish her sentence. She had marched into the jungle, looking like a soldier in her heavy boots. Then she froze, just like Rebecca had, and made a breathy, whimpering sound.

Rebecca once overheard people calling her mom *pretty*, even in her boring geologist jeans and work shirts. But right now, Mom didn't look so pretty. She didn't even look angry at Rebecca for breaking the rules.

Mom only looked scared.

Her mouth hung wide open. Her eyes were bigger than Rebecca had ever seen them. She wasn't moving… wasn't even breathing.

"Mother of god." Mom's words came out, little more than a whisper.

Rebecca whipped around and saw the thing that had frightened her mom and blocked out the sun. It was worse than all the bad dreams she'd ever had. A gross creepy-crawly jungle bug but *huge* and terrifying.

It's all my fault.

Rebecca wanted to tell her mom she was sorry for breaking the rules and going into the jungle. But she never got a chance.

A blur of gleaming insect armor and bladed legs smashed into Rebecca like a speeding freight train. Rebecca's favorite soccer ball rolled back into the clearing, dripping with dark, red blood.

FOUR

The yacht docked at the north end of the island where smiling employees greeted the guests with flowered lei.

"Welcome to Paradise!" the employees shouted in unison (Max was sure they'd rehearsed it). They then ushered Max and the others to a fleet of jeeps.

They drove inland, bouncing along a rough dirt road. The sun had gone down, but the air was still hot and smelled of wet vegetation.

As their jeeps snaked in and out of jungle clearings, more island music blared over the radio, something heavy on the ukulele. Max couldn't be sure, but it sounded like *"Tiny Bubbles"* by Don Fucking Ho. *Could they really be that cheesy?* He couldn't tell for sure. It was hard to hear the song over birds clamoring high in the trees.

A few miles south, the dirt roads gave way to paved ones and the jeeps rolled to a stop in front of the resort. The brochure had promised "Old world charm with modern amenities." As far as Max could tell, Paradise Island delivered. The main building was a sprawling French-colonial hotel with veranda-covered porches and long balconies that looked over a pristine Olympic swimming pool.

Max followed the other guests to a clearing as the staff hustled their bags to the hotel. Everyone was chatting away—a clamor of happy voices. The chatter faded when a single voice boomed above the others.

"*Bonjour, mes amis*! Hello and welcome."

The man behind the booming voice had the "handsome older gentleman" vibe down. He was tall with a lazy grace to his stroll. Mid-sixties but fit. Salt-and-pepper hair, but more salt than pepper. A tan linen suit complemented his olive skin. He smiled with his whole body.

"I am Alexander André, your honored host." The guests gathered around him, drawn in by his jovial French accent. "It is my greatest wish to make your stay on *my* island an experience you will never forget."

Max noticed he emphasized the word *my* when he said "my island"—a bit of ego creeping in his welcome speech. Between that and the Frenchman's phony gameshow host smile, Max wasn't sure he liked the guy.

André ran a hand through his wavy hair. "Whatever you need, please tell one of our staff. If you'd like a rest before dinner, your rooms have been prepared. Or feel free to visit the lounge for a drink. I recommend the Paradise Mai Tai—our signature cocktail. But be cautious. As you Americans say, they have a kick."

That earned a polite chuckle from the guests. André continued his spiel, making sweeping gestures as he spoke. "We have numerous activities for you—yoga, snorkeling, guided nature hikes. All optional, of course. But please feel free to enjoy the island's beauty at your leisure. I only ask that you stay out of the jungle preserves after sundown unless accompanied by qualified staff. We'd hate for any of you to lose your way and miss out on any fun."

As he spoke, several staff members appeared, moving with soldier-like precision. Each carried a tray loaded with champagne flutes. Chattering guests accepted the bubbly with smiles. Max waved the employee off. Champagne wasn't his thing.

"Alright, *mes amis*, enough with the rules." André lifted a flute from a passing tray and held it up for a toast. "Let us celebrate your arrival the correct way. Let your stay be paradise!"

"Fuckin' A!"

Max glanced over his shoulder and spotted the douchebag Brody, raising his flute high. His other hand rested on the shapely ass of the boat blonde. She gently guided it up to her waist.

Asshole isn't wasting any time.

Everyone tilted their elbows, taking big slurps of champagne. By the appreciative looks on their faces, it wasn't the cheap stuff.

"Now, if you'll excuse me, I have some business to attend to. But please feel free to indulge in more champagne at the lounge. Compliments of the house, of course."

The employees guided the other guests towards the poolside lounge where the bartender was already popping corks. Max hung back, sneaking a glance at André.

"What the fuck am I doing?" Max mumbled to himself. Okay, maybe he wasn't ready to date so soon after his breakup. But he could at least enjoy himself. No harm in that, right? He was in paradise, for fuck sake. But here he was, hawk-watching this André guy. Max couldn't help it. Maybe it was the Marine in him, or the bouncer. He just couldn't shake the notion that something was off with this guy.

As soon as the new arrivals shuffled away, Alexander André's demeanor changed. The cheerful host vanished. His smile faded and his eyes became cold… emotionless.

There you are, Max thought.

An engine rumbled. A jeep sped up to the resort, kicking up a cloud of dust. Its brakes squealed and a short islander slipped out from behind the wheel. He tried to keep it cool, but Max could tell he was in a hurry. He kept the jeep's engine running.

The newcomer was older than the other employees—easily mid-forties. No khaki shorts and festive tropical shirt for this guy. He wore gray cargo pants and a black polo. The clothes just screamed *"private security."*

Mr. Black Polo Shirt leaned in close to André, whispering something. The French dude's olive complexion went white. Without another word, the two of them hustled back to the jeep and sped off, heading north.

Max watched the jeep disappear around a bend, swallowed by the jungle.

Now where the fuck are you going?

FIVE

"You better not be wasting my time."

"I'm not, Mr. André." Pali gripped the wheel of the jeep and kept his eyes on the dark road that snaked through the jungle. He was a sturdy islander, short with broad shoulders and a shaved head. For three years now, he'd been the resort's head of security. Before that, Pali was a guest of Halawa Correctional Facility and wore the crude prison tats to prove it. Alexander knew him to be a *voyou*—an uneducated thug. Still, he had his uses.

The Frenchman watched the dark jungle blur by his window from the jeep's passenger seat, doing calculations in his head. "And you haven't told anyone else?"

"You know I wouldn't."

"It's just… The new construction is already millions over budget. We can't afford a hotel full of frightened guests demanding refunds right now. It would break us."

Pali glanced Alexander's way, the islander's eyes like stones. "I told no one."

Gravel crunched under the jeep's tires as it rumbled to a stop. Its headlights cut through the night, illuminating the end of the dirt road and the beach beyond. Pali put the jeep in park but didn't kill the engine. He kept the headlights on and twisted around to grab a pair of flashlights off the rear seats. They were the big Maglites, heavy enough to crack skulls.

Alexander took one of the flashlights and slipped out of the jeep. He heard the waves, surging and crashing against the shoreline below. "And you're sure we're in the right place?"

"Yes, sir. This is it."

Alexander let Pali lead him down a short embankment. As they hiked, the islander swept his flashlight over the sand. Searching.

It didn't take them long to find it.

At first sight, Alexander backpaddled and fought the urge to gasp. He didn't want to appear weak in front of his hired man.

A single foot rested on the sand like a forgotten shoe. It was bare and delicate with painted nails—a woman's foot. Dried blood caked the graying skin. A broken shin bone jutted out of jagged flesh. The break was clean, as if done by a pair of hedge clippers.

"That can't be real," Alexander said, though he could barely look at it. Moist sand filled his shoe, but he didn't care. "It's a decoration for the Americans' Halloween or a prop for the cinema."

"Afraid not, sir." Pali worked the light over the nearby sand, searching again. "One of the housekeeping staff didn't show for her shift this morning. A Tahitian girl named Mahana." Pali looked up from the sand and gazed in the direction of the jungle tree line. "There are wild pigs on the island. They aren't very big, but maybe…"

"No," Alexander said it louder than he meant to. He forced himself to look down at the severed foot.

Crabs had been at it, ripping flesh from bone. "You didn't hear me. I said that thing isn't real. In fact, we never saw it."

The Frenchman plucked up the foot by its broken shin bone and flung it far into the churning ocean. It was a stupid act. The high tide would have claimed the foot eventually. But Alexander couldn't stomach the idea of just leaving it there in the sand.

"Come back in the morning," he told Pali. "Come alone. Make sure there isn't anything else to find."

"Alright," was all Pali said before trudging up the embankment again, towards the waiting jeep. Alexander followed a few paces behind. Something in the sand caught the Frenchman's eye— something white against the moist brown sand. Alexander snatched it up and jammed it in his pocket.

They drove back to the resort in silence. This gave Alexander plenty of time to think about the white piece of plastic in his pocket—a name tag that said *Mahana*.

Alexander finally broke the stillness between them as the jeep pulled toward the big house. "Pali?"

"Yes sir?"

"Do you still have that hunting rifle?"

SIX

That dirty motherfucker drugged her drink.

It was nearly midnight. The kitschy island tunes were long gone, replaced by a DJ decked out in goggles and glowing warpaint, spinning electronic beats. Max didn't care for the Don Ho island shit. He cared for the thumping EDM crap even less.

He stood on the edge of a pavilion, squinting against the pulsing, colored lights, drinking his fourth Stella of the night. He didn't really feel much like drinking, but it went against his sacred code to refuse complementary beer. Out on the dancefloor, the YouTube douche was making a fool of himself. Brody bobbed his head with the beat as he circled packs of young ladies like they were gazelles at a watering hole. It didn't take long for him to find his prey. The young blonde had squeezed herself into a slinky red dress, with a slit up the side that showed off plenty of leg. A few minutes of consensual grinding later and the couple danced their way back to the bar.

"Two Mai Tais!" Brody shouted over the music. Waiting for their drinks, he whispered something in the girl's ear that got her giggling. His hand slid towards the slit in her dress. To her credit, the blonde tactfully and gently removed it.

Good for you, Max thought.

Brody, the self-proclaimed *Blockchain Bro*, gave her a mischievous boys-will-be-boys grin and shrugged. But his expression instantly changed when he turned his back on her to retrieve the drinks. His eyes went cold. The fun-loving party boy vanished, replaced by a predator.

Ah, shit. Max let out a heavy sigh. He'd seen that look many times working as a bouncer at the college bars. This was not going to end well.

That's when it happened. Brody slid a small vial out of his breast pocket and poured a few drops of clear liquid into one of the Mai Tais.

That dirty motherfucker drugged her drink. Max felt his blood surge. He closed the distance between himself and Brody with four big steps. His right hand balled into a fist.

A woman's voice stopped him.

"Sir!" she shouted at Brody over the music. "Sir, I can't let you have those drinks."

Brody looked up, facing the cute redhead tending bar. A sign hung behind her—palm trees arching over the words *Paradise Island* done up in green and gold neon. She wore a black cocktail dress that hugged generous curves and red lipstick. The lips smiled, but her fierce, green eyes did not. "Sir, you can't have those."

"What are you talking about?" Brody slurred his words and gave the bartender a befuddled look. He wasn't used to being called out. "These are mine. I ordered them."

"I'll make you some fresh ones."

She reached for the Mai Tais, but Brody swooped them away, out of her reach. "They're fine."

"Sir, I must insist."

The blonde beside the douchebag scrunched her eyebrows. "Brody, what's going on?"

"Do you want to tell her?" The cute bartender's lips weren't smiling anymore. She crossed her arms giving Brody a glare full of daggers.

"Bitch, I don't know what you're implying, but you're about to lose your job."

Max set his beer down. He had heard enough. He grabbed a handful of Brody's triceps—ushering him away from the bar. "Stop talking."

"Hey! Let go of me, dickwad."

Max pulled him further away from the dancefloor, digging his fingers into Brody's soft muscles. The YouTuber winced. "I'm giving you an opportunity," Max said, just loud enough to be heard over the pounding dance tunes.

"What the fuck you talking about?"

"If you walk away right now, I won't beat your ass for trying to roofie that girl's drink."

"Didn't do nothing. You kidding, why would I need roofies for a slut like that."

Max shook his head as if disappointed. He pretended to rub the stubble on his cheek, but really it was an excuse to bring his hand up to a defensive position. "Last chance."

Fueled by liquid courage, Brody's face twisted in anger. "Fuck you."

He swung on Max with a clumsy open hand. Maybe trying to humiliate him with a slap. Max stepped into the strike, blocking it with his forearm. Then he popped Brody in the nose with a short right cross. *Crack!*

Brody sat down hard on the ground, hands cupping his nose. Blood poured out of his nostrils like water from a faucet, seeping between his fingers. "I'll fucking end you for this." There was a nasal whine to his voice.

Yep, that's broken.

Brody got to his feet, threw Max one more murderous glare, then stumbled into the night. "Fucking end you!"

Max let out a heavy sigh and headed back to the pavilion bar.

So much for a relaxing night in paradise.

The blonde he'd saved from getting roofied had already made herself scarce, no doubt traumatized by the whole ordeal. But the bartender waited for him with a sly smile. She tossed him a clean bar rag.

"On a scale from one to ten," said the bartender, "how good did that feel?"

Max wiped blood from his knuckles then folded the rag and set it back on the bar. "I'm ashamed to admit, it felt pretty damn good."

And it was true. Dropping that douchebag did feel good. Almost as good as that smile the bartender flashed him.

"I'm Erin," she said, holding his gaze with those green eyes. And suddenly the night got a whole lot better.

SEVEN

Brody wondered if wandering into the jungle in the middle of the night was such a good idea. Especially after four Mai Tais, a bump of Peruvian cocaine, and a broken nose. It was the nose that distracted Brody the most, causing him to amble off the path and get lost. Even with all the booze and the drugs in his system he could feel the thing throbbing like crazy.

Fucking meathead. Brody never caught the name of the guy who smacked him. Whoever he was, bro was in a world of pain the moment he set foot stateside. Brody planned to sue his ass out of existence. Legal-fucking-Hiroshima.

Vines and brush clawed at Brody's boat shoes, as he plodded between the trees. The scent of rotting, wet vegetation hung on the cool breezes. He swept his phone's flashlight over the jungle floor.

What was that?

Something was out there in the dark. Brody couldn't see a damn thing, but he heard a rapid… *skittering*? Was that the right word? He had no idea what it could be, but he knew he didn't like the sound of it.

It struck a chord in his nervous system. Some long, forgotten instinct whispered to him, shouting at him to *"get moving bro!"*

Thank fucking Christ. Brody found the path again, illuminated by moonlight breaking through the canopy. And he saw the cell tower reach into the cloudless sky. It wasn't far. His fear of the mysterious jungle sound faded. He chuckled to himself. *Such a pussy.*

Maybe it was the Mai Tais talking or maybe he was still drunk, but Brody thought it would be a great time to livestream. He wouldn't turn the camera on himself, of course. He didn't want any of his fans seeing him with all that blood running down his nose, no doubt giving him a red beard and fucking ruining his Tommy Bahama shirt.

So instead of filming himself, he needed to give his audience something cool to look at—a killer view. That's where the cell tower came in.

Reaching the base of the tower in a clearing, Brody checked his bars. Satisfied, he hit *record* and did a slow pan of the dark riot of vegetation that surrounded him.

"Hello, crypto bitches! It is I, the great and powerful Brody, coming to you from Paradise Island."

He put on his best announcer voice, thinking he sounded cool. In his own head he couldn't hear the nasal wheezing from his broken nose.

"Not gonna lie. I'm pretty fucked up right now. So this is probably a bad decision, but here goes."

Brody aimed the camera skyward, taking in the height of the cell tower. The structure was only 65 feet tall, but from this vantage point it looked like the Eiffel Tower, a skeletal iron giant. Keeping one arm extended so he could continue to film, Brody slowly climbed the ladder welded to the side. His hands were still slick with blood from his nose and twice he almost slipped. As he ascended, Brody commented on Paradise Island, berating the amenities and staff. His livestream audience grew into the hundreds, then the thousands.

"The single ladies ain't bad. Got some hard eights strolling around in bikinis. But the staff is full of stuck-up cunts. One bartender bitch refused to serve me anymore. You believe that?"

Viewers were leaving remarks in the comments section, but Brody didn't dare peek at them, not while he was holding on to the ladder for dear life.

Finally, he reached a little work platform near the top of the tower. Sweat rolled down Brody's forehead and his breath came quick, but the ocean breezes felt cool up here. He swept his phone slowly, showing the top of the canopy and the beach beyond. Ghostly white rays of moonlight reflected off the swaying black sea.

"Not a bad view, eh boys? See how I'm risking my life to give you guys content. See how I love…"

The skittering sound cut him off. It was louder now… closer.

Brody felt his heart rev its engines. "You guys hear that?"

He leaned over the safety rail, pointing his phone at the dark canopy. The flashlight app lit up the tree tops. They swayed and shook as if something was brushing against them. Brody forgot all about the throbbing in his nose.

"What the fuck?"

The trees stopped shaking. The skittering sound fell silent. All Brody could hear was his short, shallow breaths. He was thinking this eerie silence was worse than the skittering sound. Worse than anything. Then he heard the hiss.

The tower shook. Brody almost lost hold of his phone. He grabbed hold of the railing with his free hand and held tight. Was it an earthquake?

Yeah, 'cause earthquakes make hissing noises.

The hisses grew louder. It was backed by a strange metallic drumbeat—*Cling. Cling. Cling.*

Brody turned to face the other side of the tower. In a split-second, his entire world view changed. Something was *skittering* up the skeletal tower. Something impossible.

Brody's bottom lip quivered. His phone slipped from his grasp and tumbled down into the brush below. He tried to speak, but couldn't form the words. He tried to move, but fear cemented his feet to the platform floor. The only thing he could do was piss himself.

A hundred massive insect legs raced against the tower's metal girders. The thing was a fifty-foot blur of red and black. Whip-like antenna lashed out of its horror show of a face. A horrible mouth pulsated with anticipation, its mandibles twitched, ready to rip and tear.

Brody backpaddled, slipping on a puddle of his own urine. He sat down hard on the platform's metal floor.

"Sweet mother of God."

A fraction of a second later, the freak was on him. Brody screamed as fang-like forcclaws punctured his thigh. His blood turned to acid, scorching through his veins. The pain was unimaginable. Then Brody felt nothing. His whole body seized up.

Poison! his brain screamed at him.

His muscles contracted then froze as venom surged though him. It felt like wet cement had replaced every drop of his blood. He couldn't move. Couldn't blink.

With methodical precision, the freak dragged Brody towards its waiting mouth. Inch by inch, foot by foot, the creature devoured him from the feet up. Brody could only watch it happen and listen to the sickening *crunch, crunch, crunch* of his own bones.

Before Brody's world went black, a memory flashed inside his skull. He was nine-years-old in the backyard of his stepfather's house. A dumb little kid torturing bugs. He fed grasshoppers to angry ants in a jar. He sprinkled salt on snails. He ripped the wings off butterflies.

But there was one bug he found that he would not catch—a bug that filled young Brody with a dread he could not understand—a *centipede.*

EIGHT

"I need you."

Max squinted against the morning glare and opened the sliding glass door. He had just rolled out of bed—still a little buzzed from last night's beers. "You'll have to repeat that. Just wanna make sure I'm not dreaming."

Erin, the cute bartender from the night before, stood outside the patio door of his hotel room. If she thought his line was charming, she hid it well. Her lips, which were nice and full the night before, were now a tight, flat line. Her whole vibe was somber—from the tight ponytail that restrained her long red hair to the green tank-top and hiking shorts that replaced her black cocktail dress. Still, she was damn easy to look at. Fit, but not overly muscular. A soft face and those piercing green eyes. Some nice curves and a generous pair of…

"Max." Her voice broke his train of thought. "I'm serious. I need your help."

She remembered my name.

Last night, after breaking that asshole's nose, Max tipped back a few more beers, mainly as an excuse to chat with her. He'd been telling himself he wasn't ready for dating yet, but the redhead might change his mind. Not only was she funny and damn cute, she stood up against Mr.

Douchebag with the roofies. Definitely a girl Max would like to get to know.

Unfortunately, Erin was too busy slinging complex umbrella drinks to do much talking. Max wanted to ask her to coffee or something—a first since Sharron had dumped him. But he never got a chance. No, that was a lie. Truth was, he felt awkward and self-conscious hanging around the bar all night and bailed.

Now here she was, outside his hotel room. And she *needed* him.

Max was suddenly aware he was shirtless. Normally, that wouldn't be a problem, but he hadn't worked out in months and his Marine corps physique had gone a bit soft. He grabbed a tank-top from his bag and pulled it on. "That asshole from the bar making trouble for you?"

She followed him into his hotel room, totally relaxed about it. He must've earned her trust punching out a potential sex offender. "No. In fact, nobody's heard a peep from him since last night."

"Lot of lonely ladies on the island. Maybe he met some desperate gal and hooked up."

"Jesus, did you just use the word *gal*?" Erin craned her neck, pretending to scan the room. "Where's your time machine, cowboy?"

"Sorry... Maybe he hooked up with some desperate *woman*."

Erin shook her head. "I overheard some of the staff talking. There's been no sign of him on the security cameras."

"Okay, then maybe the dickhead wandered into the jungle and fell down a hole. So sad. The douchebag community will really miss that guy."

Erin tipped her chin up, catching Max with those hard green eyes of hers. "Look, I don't care about that dickhead. I'm worried about a friend of mine and her daughter. We were supposed to meet for breakfast this morning, but they never showed up. And she's not responding to any texts."

"People forget to charge their phones all the time."

"Not Maria. She's one of those uber-organized, prepared people."

"Could she have left the island without telling you?"

"Already checked. No boats have sailed since the yacht dropped off the latest batch of guests. We've got a few fishing boats, but none of the crews have seen them."

"And you're thinking, what? Maybe she and her daughter went for a stroll and got lost?"

Erin shook her head. "The island isn't that big. And Maria knows it too well. She's a geologist, working for the resort."

Max ran a hand through his short hair, stalling for something to say. If this Maria woman didn't leave on her own and she wasn't lost, that left only a few other explanations for her disappearance. None of them were good.

"Maybe she got hurt," Erin said, breaking the quiet. "Took a fall and broke her leg? I don't know. Something just seems off about it. You ever get that feeling?"

Max nodded. "I ignored that little voice in my head a few times. Always regretted it." He reached beneath his bed and dug out his sneakers, a well-worn pair of Converse high tops. "I was going to ask you out for coffee last night," he said, "but how about we take a hike instead?"

***

Sea spray drenched the crewman as Alexander gripped the line in his gloved hands. They were aboard the resort's finest sports fishing boat, the *Monsieur Gauguin*. A young tiger shark Alexander had reeled in thrashed on the deck, still hooked. Still struggling. Still dangerous.

"Careful, Mr. Alex. She's got some fight in her yet."

"*Putain de merde!* Just keep the thing steady." Alexander held a long, serrated knife and stepped towards the shark. "And you are not to call me *Mr. Alex.* Do it again and you can look for another job."

The crewman bit his lip, nodded. "Yes sir, Mr. André."

Alexander's grip on the knife tightened and his heart began to race. This was his favorite part. The Frenchman straddled the shark, grabbed hold of its fin and began sawing. The big fish bucked and squirmed. Its mouth gaped open, showing off jagged rows of knife-edged teeth. It wanted desperately to chomp something—wanted to share its pain.

The boat bobbed over a rolling wave. Blood pooled on the wet deck, dangerously close to Alexander's suede boat shoes and the hems of his khaki pants. Alexander didn't care. The shark's fin popped loose in his grip.

Prize in hand, Alexander left the shark to its agony. He went into the deck house, shouting over his shoulder. "Toss the rest of it back in the water."

Alexander knew the crew was disgusted by this excursion. To these island people the shark wasn't a mere fish, but a sacred animal. Hunting it for its fin alone not only broke French Polynesia's ban against fishing sharks, it broke nature's law. But the men needed to feed their families, so they did what was necessary.

This made Alexander grin. Having that sort of power over these men gave him the same sense of satisfaction as cutting the fish. Later perhaps, in a rare moment of introspection, he would realize this urge to dominate the living was a product of his own insecurity. Alexander acquired his wealth the old-fashioned way: inheritance. His father had been the successful one—a poor man who built a hotel empire brick-by-brick. Alexander had achieved nothing but a fortunate birth. Every venture his father included him in had been a failure. But now, with his father's passing, Alexander had a real chance to prove himself. He had sunk much of his family's fortune into Paradise Island. If it failed, Alexander might just slit his own wrists, dive into the sea, and feed himself to the sharks.

Outside the pilothouse, two young crew members rolled the tiger shark back into the sea. It splashed and thrashed its tail on the surface before disappearing below a watery cloud of red. It would not last long down there. The other fish would soon come for it.

The way of the world.

Alexander placed the shark fin into an ice cooler and washed the blood from his hands. He gazed out a porthole. The boat's engines kicked back to life, drowning out the surf and the wind. In the distance, sitting on the horizon, was the silhouette of Paradise Island.

My island.

Minutes later, Alexander's mood soured the moment he saw Pali waiting for him on the docks. The stocky islander had traded in his resort uniform for cargo shorts, a backpack, and combat boots. He wore aviator sunglasses and held a Remington hunting rifle in a manner that suggested the gun and he were old friends.

Alexander jumped from the boat, leaving the crew to tie it to the dock. "What is it?"

"I'm afraid we have a situation, Mr. André." Pali's voice was indifferent as always. He could have been talking about the weather or ordering kung pao chicken. "Still no word on the geologist or her kid. And now we've got a guest missing too."

Alexander bit his lip to keep from screaming curses. "Who?"

"Mr. Brody. He's some sort of YouTube influencer. Does that cryptocurrency thing."

"*Merde.*" *Of all the people to go missing.*

"I don't know what's happening, boss. But maybe it is time we evacuated the island."

Alexander turned his back on Pali and faced the sea. "Impossible. If we evacuate there will no doubt be an investigation. We might even have to close for the entire season. That will ruin us." Alexander didn't mention he was deeply in debt to the Russians. If he was forced to shut down the resort, Alexander would have no way of paying their monthly "interest fees." The Popov family frowned on late payments and often sent a *monsieur* named Ivan to come collect—the kind of dead-eyed guy who kept a hatchet in the trunk of his car.

Alexander did not want a visit from Ivan.

"No," he told Pali. "We must stay open. Which means you need to keep the goddamn guests off the jungle trail."

"Already on it. We closed the trails an hour ago." Pali looked down at his combat boots. "But we do have one little problem."

Alexander closed his eyes and spoke through clenched teeth. "What now?"

"A guest and one of our employees slipped past my guys before they got a chance to close the trails. The two of them were heading north."

"Who was it?"

"Erin Johansson. She's one of our bartenders. The pretty redhead. And the guest is Max McTavish."

"A Scotsman?"

"No, he's American. According to his credit check he currently works security at a bar in Arizona."

"A fucking bouncer?" Alexander's frown deepened and a few wrinkles appeared on his brow. "How can such a man afford to stay in my resort?"

Pali shrugged. "I was about to send a crew out to find them. Our boys will…"

Alexander cut him off. "No. I want *you* to take care of it personally. Make sure they don't cause any trouble for my resort, understand?"

Pali nodded. "Yes, Mr. André," he said, then he slung the Remington over his shoulder and headed towards the jungle.

NINE

"Nice tat. You get that from the cub scouts?"

Max had thrown a cabana shirt over his tank top, but the USMC tattoo still peeked out from under the sleeve. He glanced down at it then gave the bartender a shrug. "Pretty close. I was a Marine."

"I know." Erin grinned, one eyebrow arching. "I was being facetious."

"Facetious, huh? Sounds like someone owns a thesaurus."

"I majored in English Lit at San José State. Thus the bartending career."

She had led him along a path that wove around the resort's tennis courts then hooked up with a nature trail. The trail had been well manicured at first, lined with carefully pruned flowers and painted rocks. Then it plunged into the thick foliage with a high canopy full of squawking birds. A wet, earthy scent hung in the warm air.

"So, why did you leave the Marines?" She leaned in towards him to be heard over the wildlife.

Max glanced down at his Converse sneakers, giving himself a moment to think on his answer. He considered cracking a dumb joke, which was his go-to response to personal questions. But for some reason he went with the truth.

"Got my sergeant stripes and they expected me to tell guys what to do all day. Realized I didn't like that much. Then I realized I didn't like being ordered around much either."

"So you're just a free spirit."

"Guess that's one way to look at it." Max didn't feel so free. More likely, he'd call himself aimless, bouncing from one dead-end job to the next— hanging drywall, driving an Uber, working security at a nightclub. He fought the urge to tell Erin any of this and said instead, "I did think about going back to school."

"Oh yeah? What would you study?"

"Maybe history. But what would I do with it? Can't really see me in front of a classroom."

"Wait a minute, you're telling me you're thinking about becoming an unemployed history expert?" And there went that eyebrow arch again, making Max wonder if she'd practiced it in the mirror. She couldn't keep the crooked grin from stretching across her lips. "That's a panty-dropping line to use on a first date."

Max grinned back. "First date, huh? That's what we're doing here?"

She glanced away from him, suddenly finding the jungle foliage interesting. "A singles resort doesn't seem like the kind of place for an ex-Marine," she said, changing the subject.

"Wasn't my idea. My sister booked the trip for me. She's one of those type-A people. Works as a junior executive for a marketing firm."

"Sounds like the kind of ladies who stay here."

"Exactly." A beam of sunlight cut in through the canopy and Max squinted against it. "Anyway, she and her husband are swimming in money, so they footed the bill. Guess she thought a place like this would be good for me after…" Max caught himself and his sentence trailed off.

"Uh, oh," said Erin. "Is that drama I sense?"

"Had a bad break up a couple of months ago."

Erin stopped along the path, shielding her eyes against the sun so she could look at him. "How bad are we talking here?"

"I bought her a ring. She gave it back to me."

"Oof. Sorry, man."

"It's for the best," Max said, but his voice didn't sound all that convincing, even to himself. One of those awkward silences hung between them and he gazed down at his feet again. That's when he spotted the prints in the dirt. One pair of tracks, made by casual deck shoes, not hiking boots.

"I think I got something," he said, crouching down.

"Excellent work, Marine," Erin said, punching him in the tattoo. She dug out a bottle and applied more sunscreen. Curse of the redhead. "Appears you've found a shoe print on a dirt trail."

Max gazed up at her. He hadn't noticed the spray of freckles across her nose before, or how deeply green her eyes were. "Look closer, smartass," he said, nodding at the ground. "See how the footsteps have a wobbly pattern. Like a stumbling drunk would make. That sound like anyone to you?"

"The guy with the roofies? Brody something?"

"He'll always be Senor Douchebag to me. If I'm right, he headed this way after I popped him."

"Let's find out." Her body brushed against his as she pushed ahead of him on the trail. The women in his life often referred to Max as a *good guy*, but he couldn't help but glance at her ass as she led the way.

He followed the ass along a path that snaked its way into a dense stand of tropical trees where the high canopy provided little shade from the mid-morning sun. Max wiped a line of perspiration from his forehead. If it wasn't for the cool, salty breezes sweeping in from the shore, he'd be sweating buckets.

Birds and insects filled the underbrush, unseen but not unheard. They created a jungle soundtrack of chirping and buzzing. Max slapped the back of his neck, squashing a mosquito. He almost bumped into Erin who had stopped in her tracks at the edge of a clearing.

She stood frozen, peering into the clearing. "What the hell happened here?"

Max followed her gaze. The island's cell tower stood at the center of the clearing. At sixty feet high, its top still barely peeked over jungle canopy. *Something* had battered the cell tower's antenna panels and twisted the pipes housing its routing cables. That same *something* had bent many of the thick metal bars that made up the tower's skeletal frame. And was it his imagination or had the vegetation been trampled? Like a jeep had plowed through the dense undergrowth.

"What could've done that?" Erin shaded her eyes and gazed up at the tower. "You think someone climbed up there and took a crowbar to it?"

"I don't think so." Stepping into that clearing, Max felt a sense of creeping unease. It was a feeling he was familiar with, having cultivated it while running patrols in Kabul gunning for insurgents. He approached the cell tower with his head on a swivel, scanning the jungle for threats.

A few feet from the tower's base, Max caught a glimpse of something shiny amongst a thick growth of bushes. It was a cell phone, tangled in the plant's branches. Max was about to pick it up, then stopped himself. He recognized blood splattered across the phone's screen.

"Ah, jeez. That isn't jelly, is it?"

Max shook his head. More blood marked the frame of the tower, the red stains beginning to go brown under the tropical sun.

"You did smash his nose up pretty good. Maybe that's why it's bloody."

"Could be," said Max.

"You could try sounding more convinced."

"I don't like lying to people." Max squatted down close to the base, inspecting the blood stains and a series of deep scratches in the metal. That's when he noticed the strange tracks. They were sharp holes gouged in the dirt like spear points—a few inches in diameter. There were dozens of them, lined up in near perfect parallel lines.

What the fuck?

Being a redhead, Erin was already on the pale side. Now, she appeared ghost white. "I don't like this."

To the left of the tower, a tall clump of bushes trembled, its leaves rustling. Max tensed up.

There was something moving around over there.

A man stepped out from the bushes—the island's head security guy, Pali, holding a hunting rifle with a scope attached. The muzzle wasn't pointed at Max, but it wasn't pointed away from him either.

"The trails are closed." Pali's voice was cold and distant. "You shouldn't be here."

"What's with the rifle?" Max stepped in front of Erin, putting his body between her and the Remington's barrel.

Pali shrugged. "We've got a wild pig population on the island. Mostly, they're harmless. But occasionally they'll charge you. And we wouldn't want that to happen to any of our esteemed guests. So let's go now, yes?"

Max gestured to the damaged cell tower. "You think pigs did that? Good climbers, these pigs?"

The stocky islander opened his mouth to reply, but didn't have an answer. Not once did he survey the damage or inspect the blood stains.

Because he's already seen them. He knows something.

"And we found blood on the metal," Erin said. "We think one of the guests got hurt."

Pali gave her a smug half-smirk. "And here I thought you were just a bartender. All this time we had a great detective slinging beers."

"Not great," said Erin. "But good enough to notice those cheap prison tattoos running up your arm."

Pali's smirk died. "You want to keep your job, girl?"

"Honestly, I don't give a shit." Her voice was calm, without heat. "I'm just trying to find my friend Maria and her girl. You hear any word from them?"

Pali sighed as he rolled his neck like a boxer warming up for a fight. He ignored Erin's question and target locked Max with a hard stare. "It's time for you and Miss Johansson to return to the resort."

Erin, hands on her hips, returned his stony gaze. "Well, I think it's time for you to go fu… "

A shrill screech cut Erin off. The sound was distant, echoing through the trees. Still it was undeniable.

Someone was screaming.

TEN

"Jesus, what's a girl gotta do to get laid around here?"

Tiffany stomped angrily across a white sandy beach and down the wooden dock towards a cluster of bungalows on stilts over the lagoon. These were the high-ticket suites. She'd paid a small fortune for it—all of it out her daddy's bank account—and she intended to get *his* money's worth.

Sure the place was nice. She liked the island nicknacks on the walls—the little tiki totems and the Gauguin prints. She liked the hardwood floors too, with the glass observation window letting you watch the tropical fish frolicking below your feet. But Tiffany wasn't here for fish. She was here to hunt. And her prey was one Augustine Barnes.

Augie was a superstar financial analyst for a high-profile fortune 500 company. His income was seven figures. He owned properties in Manhattan, Miami, and on Coronado Island. Okay, so he wasn't the best-looking bachelor at the resort. At thirty-one, his hair was already thinning. He was maybe five foot seven with thick glasses, and he had a Jell-O gut instead of a six-pack. But in Tiffany's eyes, those seven-figures of his made him a Hemsworth.

Earlier that morning, she had tried to take him down while they were sipping post-yoga pineapple smoothies together. After showing off her downward dog for thirty minutes, she laughed at his lame jokes, feigned interest in his office stories, and even did the forearm touch three times. Three! Either Augie was too dense to pick up on her advances or too pathetically shy to do anything about them.

"There's a third option," said the little voice in the back of her head. *"Maybe he wasn't into you. Maybe he liked that blonde bitch better."*

The blonde bitch in question was a slut named Belinda or Malinda or some such nonsense. Tiffany had spotted her at their morning yoga class, giving her Augie a heavy dose of "fuck me" eyes. How dare she move in on Tiffany's kill? Sure, Tiffany's tits weren't as big as this Malinda's (why were so many dudes into that anyway?). But Tiffany knew her face was cuter, and Pilates and spin classes had done her body good. It was a verified fact she looked smoking hot in these skintight yoga pants. There was no chance Augie would pick the blonde bitch over her. *Was there?*

She would just have to set out better bait to seal the deal.

Tiffany knew Augie would be passing by her bungalow any minute now to get to his own. On his way, he'd get an eyeful of Tiffany lounging on her suite's patio getting some sun in her brand-new string bikini. Yeah, that would stop the nerd in his tracks. Then she'd invite him in for a drink and pounce.

Quickly, Tiffany shimmied out of her yoga pants and slipped into the three tiny pieces of fabric she called a swimsuit. She checked the mirror to see if her makeup needed any touch-ups (yes, she wore makeup to yoga class, duh). Then she grabbed her sunglasses and dashed out to the patio area. She considered lying on her back, which was more suggestive. But there was a chance Augie wouldn't see her as he walked by. So she sat on the lounger instead, one leg bent, head tipped back ever so slightly.

Yeah, that'll do it.

"You sure?" asked the little voice. *"I mean, a bikini isn't exactly a showstopper at a tropical resort. Every girl on the island wears a bikini."*

"Damn it, you're right."

Tiffany quickly ripped off her top and flopped back down on the lounger, trying to look sexy as fuck but also nonchalant. She knew from experience that guys *always* stopped for tits, even if they weren't the biggest in the world.

Her knockoff Ferragamo sunglasses didn't do shit to screen out the UVs, so she closed her eyes and waited.

It wasn't long before Tiffany heard the patter of flip-flops on the boardwalk, coming closer. This was it. Time to spring the trap.

"Oh, hey there, Augie. I didn't know you were headed this…"

It wasn't Augie.

Instead, a resort employee—a tall islander guy—stood there holding a tower of folded towels. The guy didn't move a muscle, just gawked awkwardly at her, like he had been shot by a freeze ray.

"Ahhh, sorry Miss. I bring towels. Do you like any towels?"

"No. I'm fine. Just get out of here, please. You'll ruin everything."

"Yes, ma'am," said the guy. But he didn't move. Didn't blink.

"Now, please."

"Oh yes. Of course, ma'am."

The islander shook himself out of his trance, turned tail, and headed back the way he came. Tiffany smiled.

Guess the bait is working.

As a rule, Tiffany always checked out a young guy's ass as they walked away. So she lowered her shades and watched towel boy scamper across the beach with his towels. *Not bad.* The guy's baggy cargo shorts couldn't hide the fact he worked on his glutes. Definitely didn't skip the squats at the gym.

Maybe if it doesn't work out with Augie, I'll pay him a visit and...

A hissing rattle filled Tiffany's ears. Then the beach exploded, sending up a violent plume of white sand. Without uttering a word, towel boy vanished.

Like the earth swallowed him whole.

Unconsciously, Tiffany got to her feet and reached for her bikini top. She was too confused to be scared, but she felt vulnerable.

"Towel boy?"

Everything went quiet. The gulls stopped their squawking. Bugs stopped their buzzing. Even Tiffany held her breath. Only the gentle lapping of waves against the dock posts remained.

She heard the hiss again.

Tiffany backed up, edging toward the bungalow door. She got three steps before witnessing a second volcanic burst of sand. As the sand rained down, a massive shape blurred towards her—a huge, hideous centipede, longer than a bus. Its twitching mandibles were coated with bloody sand.

Tiffany let out a string of screams, bellowing louder and louder. She turned to run but was slammed in the back by a freight train. A shock of pain, sharper than anything she'd ever felt, rippled through her body. Her spine snapped with the impact.

The creature scooped Tiffany up with those grotesque mandibles, hoisting her off her feet. With her spine shattered, Tiffany couldn't feel the incredible pressure exerted on her hips. But she *could* hear the sickening *SHHHLUNKK* of her body being clipped in two.

Before the merciful void claimed her, Tiffany looked down and saw the bottom half of her body lying on the dock. The legs kicked and quivered as blood gushed out of her severed waist. Then the mandibles began their work, shoveling Tiffany's torso into the creature's eager mouth.

ELEVEN

"That's not fucking real, is it?"

It was Erin asking the question, her eyes wide with disbelief. The three of them stared down at the severed hand lying on the boardwalk. It was a woman's hand. Shards of the ulna and radius jutted out from torn, ragged flesh. A pool of blood had formed beneath the severed limb, staining both bone and skin. The blood was fresh.

Max crouched down, getting a better look. When they heard the screams, he'd sprinted alongside Erin and the security guy all the way to the resort bungalows. Max hadn't run like that since the corps. Hot blood raced through his veins as his heart pounded away.

But now, his blood ran cold.

"That's no Halloween decoration." He watched the blood stream away from the severed hand to the edge of the boardwalk. It dripped down into the seawater that surged gently beneath the docks.

"Ah Jesus." Erin covered her mouth and turned away. "Oh, shit."

Max squinted up at the security guy. "Your pigs do this?"

Pali the security guy didn't answer. His face was a stone.

"We should look for the rest of the body," Max said, standing up.

"You won't find it." Pali scanned their surroundings, the rifle held low. But Max noticed that his grip on the weapon had tightened.

Erin spun around, facing him. A hot ferocity came to life in her green eyes. "And why the hell not?"

Pali's gaze never wavered. He surveyed the area like an owl, searching for prey. "Whatever this is only leaves scraps."

Erin stepped towards him. "So you knew about this? You knew and didn't tell the guests... the staff? What about Maria?"

Max placed a hand on her shoulder, easing her away. "Come on, Erin. Let's get back to the resort. We've got to warn the others."

He ushered her along the boardwalk, towards the beach. They made it a few yards before Pali called out to them.

"I can't let you do that."

Max didn't need to look at the man to know he'd raised the rifle. He knew too that there was a round already chambered. Slowly, Max turned. He held his hands out to the side where the security guy could see them. "You willing to shoot us?"

"Don't want to."

"But you will."

Pali shrugged. "Maybe I'll tie you up instead. Stash you away in the storage shed over there."

Max took a careful step towards the islander. If the guy let him get close enough, Max planned on rushing him. Maybe he could knock the dude off the dock, send him splashing into the water below before he could get a shot off. It was a hell of a *maybe*, but what else could Max do?

"That's close enough," said Pali. He eased his finger into the rifle's trigger guard.

"Sure," said Max. But he took another step anyway.

"I mean it, white boy. You take one more step and I'll put you in the ground."

Max didn't get a chance to reply. Behind Pali, something erupted out of the once calm sea, throwing up a massive spout of water in the air. Something huge that let out a horrific hiss.

Three words burst from Max's mouth as he backed away. "Holy fuck balls!"

The *something* that had burst from the water was a nightmarish centipede of monstrous proportions—more than four feet wide and who-the-fuck-knew how long. Most of its segmented body still slithered beneath the water's surface. It lurched forward, snatching Pali up with its mandible-like foreclaws. Pali, the ex-con tough guy, screamed like an eight-year-old girl as the creature lifted him toward its unholy mouth and...

CRUNCH... CRUNCH... CRUNCH...

Erin's eyes went wild and wide. A wave of cold panic rippled across her face, but she couldn't turn away. "It's eating his skull."

Max whispered, not wanting to gain the creature's attention. "Erin..."

"Eating his skull... Like a tootsie pop."

"Erin, back away. Slowly."

She gave him the smallest nod in the world and they each took one shaky baby step backwards.

Pali's legs spasmed and kicked uncontrollably as the creature's mandibles shoveled more of his body into its waiting mouth.

Just a reflex, thought Max. *He's dead already. Please let him be dead.*

Mandibles sunk into Pali's stomach, popping it like a blood-fattened tick. Guts and gore spewed out, dribbling down the centipede's legs. The monster bug didn't seem to mind, and kept chomping away.

"Go, now!"

Erin took a few clumsy steps backwards then spun and broke into a full-tilt sprint. Max charged close behind her, listening for the monster. He knew when it stopped crunching away on the security dude, it was their turn. He also knew they'd never outrun that thing. Too many damn legs. So when Max saw the bungalow with its wide open door, he made a choice.

"What're you doing?" Erin stumbled forward as Max gave her a hard shove towards the bungalow.

"Get inside and find some cover."

"What about you?"

Max said nothing. He pulled the bungalow door shut and dashed back towards the monstrosity at the end of the dock. As he ran, his eyes frantically swept across the wooden pathway.

Where is it? Where the fuck is it?

He found what he was looking for near the edge of the boardwalk—the security guy's hunting rifle. He snatched the Remington up just as Pali's feet disappeared into the monster bug's twitching, bloody mouth. Finished with its first course, the creature looked down at Max with a cluster of dark, dead eyes.

Max swung the rifle up, took quick aim, and squeezed the trigger. A bullet rang harmlessly off the creature's armored face.

"Shit."

As if responding to his curse, the creature let out a horrible, rattling *HISSSSSSSSS*.

Max ran.

TWELVE

Erin stood frozen inside the bungalow, staring at the closed door in disbelief. Her heart pounded so rapidly, it felt like it would rupture.

This isn't happening.

A second ago, that Max guy had shoved her inside and slammed the door shut. It didn't matter that they barely knew each other—he was risking his own life to save hers.

Gotta do something. Can't just let him die out there.

She reached for the doorknob with trembling fingers. Maybe she could convince Max to hide in here with her. Maybe they'd be safe from that thing.

A gunshot rang out followed by a horrible hissing noise. It was like nothing Erin had ever heard before. Primal and angry, yet almost mechanical.

Erin forgot all about the door. In a daze, she slowly backed away. A tremor of fear rippled through her body. Her heel caught the edge of a rug, and she stumbled, flopping down hard on her ass.

Fucking hell!

Erin rolled off the rug and found herself on all fours, staring through a thick pane of glass built into the bungalow's floorboards. Erin figured it was so resort guests could stare down at tropical fish frolicking in the clear water below. But there was no frolicking going on at the moment. Any fish down there were rightly scared shitless and staying away. Erin knew how they felt.

Too afraid to open the door, she rushed to a window on the other side of the bungalow. She peered out just in time to see Max, gripping the dead guy's hunting rifle and running for his life down the dock.

He's leading that freak away.

She felt a flood of relief followed by a stab of guilt. She might just get out of this alive, but at what cost?

Max...

He has the rifle now. Maybe he can...

No. Erin knew she was lying to herself. That rifle might've been able to drop a deer or an elk, but against that thing? No way. Max was as good as...

BOOM!

Erin's whole world shook. She staggered, almost falling to the floor again. It felt like a monster truck had just smashed into the side of the bungalow. But it wasn't a truck.

It's trying to get in here... Trying to get me!

Another BOOM rocked the little cottage. Its foundations trembled, dislodging tacky decorations from the wall. Tiki statues and Matisse prints crashed against the hardwood. Erin saw something lying there with the other nicknacks and plucked it up off the floor.

It was a native spear that had been hanging on the wall—decorative to be sure, but still imposing with its eight-inch blade bristling with shark teeth. Desperate, Erin gripped it tightly, held her breath, and waited for the thing to crash its way inside.

***

Max never ran so hard in his life. One second, he was taking aim at the huge centipede monster. The next second, he found himself nearly 200 feet away, on the other side of the boardwalk—the bungalows nothing but a passing blur. Any moment, he expected to feel sharp mandibles shank their way into his ribcage.

But the pain never came.

Max risked throwing a glance over his shoulder. Instead of chasing him, the monstrosity stopped at the bungalow where he'd stashed Erin. The creature's massive antenna slashed the air, hammering down on the bungalow's roof. Then the thing reared back and slammed its armored head into the building's side. The entire dock shuddered with the impact.

No, damn it. The freak knows she's in there.

Chambering another round, Max brought the rifle up and fired. He knew it wouldn't do any good, but what else could Max do? His bullet sparked off the monster's hide again. The freak didn't even notice it had been shot.

"Get away from there, you bastard!" Max worked the bolt and fired again.

This time, the creature skittered backwards, its spear-like legs clicking against the dock. For a moment, Max thought he actually hurt the thing.

Then he realized it was just giving itself some room to build up momentum. The massive bug shot forward, a terrifying blur of insectile armor. It bulled into the bungalow again with a thunderous boom. All the building's windows exploded and a spiderweb of cracks rippled across its walls. One more crash like that and the building would come tumbling down.

Desperate, Max dashed back towards the creature, working the bolt on the gun. He knew this particular Remington was a hunting model with only a four-round magazine. Which meant he only had one bullet left. Max wasn't sure what to do until he spotted the barbecue grill on one of the bungalow's patios.

His adrenaline surging, Max quickly unhooked the grill's propane tank and ripped it free. Maybe he could drive this fucker away with fire.

But he was too slow. The gigantic bug smashed into the bungalow a third time, using its head like a battering ram. Walls burst with the impact, sending out a wave of flying shrapnel—bricks, plaster, shards of wood.

Max didn't see Erin among the refuse. He didn't need to. The bungalow looked as if someone had dropped a bomb on it. Max knew nothing could've survived that.

The creature circled the wreckage. Its whip-like antenna twitched as it searched for its dead prey. With a grunt, Max flung the propane tank. It bounced twice and skidded across the boardwalk before rolling under the creature's body.

Max clenched his teeth together. He wanted to scream an onslaught of curses. Instead, he brought the rifle to his shoulder. Holding his breath a beat, he exhaled as he pulled the trigger. The Remington let out a loud crack.

VOOOOSH! His bullet hit home. The canister erupted spewing out a flash of fire. The explosion knocked the creature backwards, blowing off two of its legs. Its furious hiss reverberated off the dock. Putrid smoke rose from its charred exoskeleton. It uncoiled, standing tall like a cobra, its eyes fixing Max with a deadly glare.

Max didn't back away. Didn't run. There was no use. The freak still had plenty of legs left to propel it across the boardwalk.

Can't believe this is how I go out.

He lowered the empty Remington and waited for the monster to come.

***

When the canister erupted, Erin was standing in waist-high seawater just below a pile of wreckage formerly known as the bungalow. Thirty seconds before, she had used the decorative spear to bust through the observation glass in the floorboard. And not a moment too soon. Screaming obscenities, she dropped down into the water just as the freak smashed through the building like a coked-up freight train.

Now, Erin stood trembling between the bungalow's stilts, gripping the spear and staring up through the observation port. With the bungalow gone, she had a clear view of the sky above. It was a gentle blue—clear, calm, and beautiful. Erin was convinced it was the last thing she'd ever see.

Hail, Mary, full of grace. The lord is... Oh, fucking Christ... How does the rest of it go?

Up on the boardwalk, the creature hissed again as it charged. Its spiked legs clawed the deck furiously, sending a shudder down Erin's spine. Her hidey hole went suddenly dark. It was the freak... running right past the observation window, blocking out the sunlight.

Erin didn't know why she did it. Maybe it was some primitive, monkey-brained survival instinct screeching at her. *Kill! Kill! Kill!*

Erin followed orders and tightened her grip on the spear as she thrust it straight up at the passing creature. Her blade bit deep into the bug's soft underbelly. It would've been a superficial stab if not for one thing—the freak kept running. Momentum carried the creature forward and Erin's spear opened up its guts like a zipper. Its bug belly burst wide, showering Erin with red and purple slime with a consistency of *thick n' chunky* salsa.

"Fuuuuuuuuuuck!"

Erin gagged as the slime ran down her face and oozed between her tightly-clenched lips. The goo had an overwhelming sickly-sweet stench to it, like rotting pork. But she never let go of the spear. Not until the bug had passed by overhead, out of sight. Erin could see blue skies again.

***

Max watched the monstrosity lurch forward then do a king-sized face plant. The boardwalk cracked and shook on its stilts. Black smoke rose from the creature's burnt exoskeleton, and vile goo also oozed from its underbelly, spilling out by the gallons. The freak's massive head drooped down. Its mandibles and legs went full on spaz mode, twitching wildly. Then everything stopped, like someone had switched off the creature's power.

Max took one wary step towards the thing. He gripped the dead man's rifle even though its magazine was empty.

You better stay fucking dead.

Max let out a long breath as the adrenaline seeped out of him. He paced across in front of the bungalows, unsure what to do with himself. So many questions buzzed inside his skull. *What was this thing? Where did it come from? What now?*

Then he remembered Erin and his chest felt like it was full of wet cement. She was under the rubble, somewhere. Was there a chance she still clung to life?

No. If Max knew one thing it was that hope was a losing game. Erin was dead. The freak had smashed through that little bungalow like a wrecking ball. Nobody could've survived that. Nobody…

"Hey! A little help here?"

A fresh surge of adrenaline coursed through Max's veins. He spun, scanning the wreckage. A hand poked out of the rubble of the bungalow, waving at him.

THIRTEEN

"Our first date and I already got your clothes off."

Erin let out an exhausted laugh. "You're fucking hilarious."

Erin stood in the bungalow's bathtub, wearing nothing but her bra and panties. The shower sprayed down on her, washing away the jelly-like bug guts that stuck to her skin and hair.

The shower was Max's idea.

He had found her under the boardwalk, standing in waist-high salt water with her spear—the cute bartender not looking so hot all drenched in putrid, purple goo. She splashed herself frantically, saying the slime wasn't coming off. Worse yet, it was starting to burn. Max pulled her up from the observation port, resisting the urge to sweep her up in a bear hug. Instead, he ushered Erin through the rubble, kicked open the door to another bungalow, and helped her strip off her clothes.

Max had one thought on his mind, and it wasn't sex. Who knew what was in that freak's stomach? Maybe some mega gastric acid or some deadly bacterial shit. They needed to get it off Erin's skin, immediately. So he shoved her into the bathroom and turned the shower on full blast.

Now, after watching Erin rinse the goop away for the past five minutes, Max had to admit, she looked damn good all wet. She arched her back under the shower stream, washing her face and slicking her hair against her wet skin. Mother Nature had gifted her with full breasts that filled out that black bra of hers. It was hard to take his eyes off her, but Max tried.

He washed his hands and forearms in the sink beside the tub, stealing quick glances.

Erin noticed and flashed him a crooked smirk. "I think I got it from here, cowboy."

Now it was Max's turn to grin. "You sure? You've been through a lot. Maybe you shouldn't be alone right now."

"You're a saint."

Max shrugged. "Just looking out for you, ma'am."

"Oh, I've noticed you're doing a lot of looking."

Max looked down, as if he'd suddenly found the tile floor fascinating. "Yeah. Sorry about that."

"Don't be. Normally, I wouldn't mind. But I just watched a gigantic centipede eat a man alive. Yeah, he seemed like a dick, but he was still a human being. Doesn't seem appropriate to flirt after that, you know?"

"Guess you're right. I'll find you some clothes." He was almost through the bathroom door then turned back. "Hey Erin?"

"Yeah?"

"Glad you're not dead."

She gave him a full-fledged smile this time. "I'm glad you're not dead too. Now get out of here."

Max shut the bathroom door behind him and began hunting around the bedroom for something

Erin could wear. Luckily, the single who rented the bungalow was a woman, and close to the bartender's size. Max found a pair of capri shorts and a button-up blouse hanging in the closet. He considered searching for a bra and some panties too, but it felt weird swiping other people's underwear.

Way too pervy.

He was laying the dry clothes out on the bed when he heard Erin scream. And it wasn't a *the-shower-went-cold* scream. It was more like a *I'm-gonna-fucking-die* type scream. Max bolted back to the bathroom and reached for the door.

"Erin?"

She screamed again and Max barged into the little room. She was fully nude now, having dropped her soaked underwear on the floor. But Max barely noticed her body. He was too focused on the two-foot mutant centipede Erin was wrestling with.

The creature hissed as Erin held it as far away from her torso as she could. Its claws dug into her forearm, drawing blood. Erin clenched her teeth together and held tight. The thing twisted in her grasp, trying to get at her with its clicking mandibles.

Max grabbed hold of the centipede's tail end with both hands. He looked Erin in the eyes. "I got it. Let go!"

The split-second Erin loosened her grasp, Max swung the creature as hard as he could, bashing it against the sink basin. Insectile armor gave way with a crunch, but the freak still hissed.

Max swung it again, and again.

"Die, you motherfucker! Die!"

The porcelain cracked and bug guts splattered the mirror. Finally, the thing stopped squirming... Stopped hissing.

Max slumped against the bathroom wall, trying to catch his breath. "Where the hell did that come from?"

"The window. It was only open a few inches, but..." Erin's words trailed off. She quickly wrapped a long towel around herself, shaking her head. Her whole body trembled. "I think it was... It was..."

"Jesus, don't say it."

"I think it was a baby."

"Shit." Max pushed himself off the wall. "You know what that means, don't you?"

Erin pulled the towel tighter and nodded. "This isn't over."

FOURTEEN

Out on the docks, Max found a small storeroom attached to one of the guest bungalows. It was basically a deep closet full of fresh towels, toilet paper, and cleaning supplies. Everything the housekeeping staff needed to clean and restock the suites. Max dug out a pair of latex gloves, then grabbed some plastic garbage bags. He fastened the bags around his Converse sneakers, pulled on the gloves, and went to work.

Trudging to the carcass, Max listened to his trash-bag-covered sneakers scraping and whooshing across the dock planks. The stench hit him from yards away—the overpowering sickly-sweet scent of rotting flesh.

Why in the fucking world do dead things smell sweet?

The creature itself was a twisted playground sculpture, its lifeless exoskeleton like something children would clamber all over, zooming down its long legs as if they were jungle gym slides. Only the burn marks and blood-dripping mandibles ruined the image.

"Lets get this fucking over with," Max muttered to himself. He held his breath, clamping his teeth together tightly. His stomach churned.

A deep puddle of gore trailed behind the monstrosity, marking its path from the demolished bungalow to the foot of the docks. The sludge had the look and viscosity of Vaseline, yet with floating chunks of bloody meat. Max followed the grizzly trail, skirting around the muck without stepping into it. It took a minute of scanning the gore to find the security guy's remains.

Max had witnessed men blown apart by RPGs and shot to Hell with AK-47s, but he'd never seen anything like this. He shook his head in disbelief. The security goon had been chomped into segmented pieces, as if it had been systematically cut in a factory. The gore splattered body parts floated in the goop of bug innards, not yet dissolved by digestion. Max spotted the guy's shredded backpack next to his severed head. Thankfully, it was face down, so Max didn't have to look into its dead eyes.

Max gagged and fought down a stream of bile. He was about to slog into the muck when a voice stopped him.

"Hey, hold on a sec."

Erin jogged to him in her borrowed running shoes, holding a small plastic bottle of hand sanitizer. Her nose was crinkled and she squinted against the oppressive smell.

"Jesus, that's awful." She pumped a generous amount of sanitizer on to her hand then leaned towards Max and applied a smear just below his nostrils. As she did so, her soft fingertips brushed gently against his lips. They shared a look and somehow, the moment felt more intimate to Max than their time in the shower.

"What's that for?" he asked.

"It's to cover up the smell." Erin rubbed some of the sanitizer under her own lip. "I saw this on one of those CSI type shows. Except I think they used Vapo Rub."

At a loss for words, Max nodded and took in a breath. Immediately, the harsh alcohol scent made his eyes water. Not a pleasant sensation, but Erin was right. It helped cut the putrid dead smell.

"Can't believe I'm doing this," said Max, then he trudged into the thick trail of bug guts. He took a few tentative steps, feeling the liquefied innards slosh against his ankles. Damn, was he thankful for the trash bags wrapped around his sneakers. The oozing blood was turning the bug sludge pink here. Max ignored his own churning guts, hunched, and lifted the backpack from a puddle of gore. Slime dripped from the ripped fabric.

They better be fucking in there, Max thought.

"Any luck?" Erin called out to him from her spot, several feet away from the gore trail.

Max flashed her a smile as he pulled out a box of .308 Winchester rounds. He felt dumb, grinning in such grisly circumstances, but he couldn't help it. "Looks like we're in business."

Max's grin faded. He noticed Erin freeze in place, her piercing eyes locked on something behind him. She did not gasp or shrink back in horror, but her lower lip began to tremble. Max turned and saw a single pink sneaker floating among the innards—a child's shoe, splashed with blood. And there was something beyond the shoe, something floating in the muck. Max's brain desperately wanted to reject what he was seeing.

"Rebecca," Erin whispered.

Max didn't need to be told this was the little girl they'd been searching for. He stepped in front of Erin, blocking her view.

"Don't look," he said, even though it was too late. Erin would never be able to shake what she had just seen. It would haunt her until she took her last breath. Max wrapped his arms around her and pulled her into a hug. She fought him at first, then sunk into his chest.

"Oh God. Oh God. That means Maria… "

"Come on, let's get you out of here."

Erin struggled out of his grasp, glaring up at him. "No, we can't just leave her. We have to…"

She never got to finish her sentence. Violently, the giant centipede's carcass shuddered as if hit with 50,000 volts. Its legs twitched and thrashed. A loud hiss rattle shook the docks. One thought raced through Max's mind.

Oh fuck. It's still alive!

***

Alexander was on his way back from the north docks when he heard the explosion. Instinctively, he hit the brakes and his jeep skidded to a dusty stop along the dirt road. A crossroads sat beyond his windshield. One road led to the main resort. The other wound its way to the east dock where the private bungalows were located.

The Frenchman sat still behind the wheel, listening, but he heard nothing else. Moments before the explosion, he thought he had heard two distant cracks that sounded suspiciously like gunshots. But his mind dismissed them as construction sounds from the work site.

There was no dismissing the explosion.

Alexander grabbed the walkie-talkie from the passenger seat and tried to reach Pali again. No luck. Only static.

Damn that bastard. Why didn't he answer?

Alexander felt his grip tighten on the wheel. The Frenchman knew he was not a brave man, but more than anything he feared the loss of his wealth. He had to protect his investments, no matter the risk.

He yanked the wheel hard and the jeep rumbled on the road, heading in the direction of the bungalows.

FIFTEEN

HISS!

The dock bucked sending the ex-marine stumbling backwards into the sludge with a splash. Wet slime spurted up in his wake, spraying his face.

Gaaaaaah!

Like a crab, he scuttled backwards, away from the giant bug. Somehow, amid all the chaos, he made the realization that the hiss the monster had been making wasn't coming from its mouth. It was the sound its legs made as they rubbed against each other. A horrible, insectile music.

Rifle! Got to get to the rifle!

Erin had fallen backwards too and was now scrabbling in the sand beside the dock. By the time they both got to their feet, a spasm rippled through the massive centipede and its enormous body flopped back down. A new outpouring of goo oozed out from its underbelly sloshing down the docks, a wave of white putrid jelly.

"Christ, that scared the shit out of me." Max's heart was a jackhammer inside his chest. He turned away from the gush of white innards that spewed out of the freak's guts. "If that fucker wasn't dead before, it is now. You figure those were its death throes or something?"

Erin didn't reply. Her face was carved in ice. Without a word, she stormed towards the creature, stopping only to scoop up a long piece of broken lumber off the ground—shrapnel from the demolished bungalow. Rearing back, she swung the lumber like a bat. Wood collided with the centipede's armored head, sending splinters flying. Erin swung again and again, cursing and grunting with each strike. The lumber rang off the exoskeleton with a *clack, clack, clack*. It barely left a mark.

Max didn't try to intervene. He watched her swing away at the creature until her arms went slack with exhaustion. Chest heaving, she let her club slip out of her grasp and thump against the dock. Much of her fiery red hair had worked free from its ponytail and hung wildly in front of her face.

"Somehow, I knew they were gone." Her voice was calm now, almost subdued. She wiped a stream of tears from her face with the back of a forearm. "But seeing Rebecca like that... Guess I just lost it."

"You're entitled," said Max. "I'm so sorry, Erin. I wish we could've done something for them."

"Me too." Erin nodded. Then she was looking over her shoulder, down at the sand. Something had caught her eye. "Too bad we don't have time to grieve for them now."

"Why's that?"

"You remember the little bastard that attacked me in the bathroom?" Erin nodded her chin towards the beach line surrounding the docks. Max followed her gaze.

Strange tracks wove through the sand, up a berm, and into the jungle—pairs of perfect lines, poked into the ground by hundreds of sharp spikes.

Baby freaks.

Max tried to figure out how many separate trails there were, but lost count. "There must be hundreds of them."

"Yeah," said Erin. "And I'll give you one guess where they're headed."

Before Max could respond, the grinding roar of an engine caught his attention. One of the resort jeeps barreled out from the jungle path and into the clearing thirty feet from the docks. Its brakes squealed and its tires kicked up a plume of sand.

Alexander André, the resort's owner, cut the engine but didn't step out from behind the wheel. The jeep had an open top, and the Frenchman stood up in a daze, staring over the windshield. If he noticed Max and Erin approaching the vehicle, he didn't show it. André's wide eyes were locked on the centipede's monstrous carcass sprawled across the dock. A few seagulls had swooped down from the sky, perching themselves on the thing's back, squawking to each other. Max wondered if they were drawn by the rotting fish smell that rose from the dead creature in putrid waves. The godawful stench tainted the warm tropical breezes.

"It's dead?" André's voice was little more than a whisper.

"That's right," said Erin. "We killed the fuck out of it." There was no heat in her tone, but a cold fury came to life in her eyes.

Max gestured with the rifle. "But not before it chowed down on your security guy."

André shook his head again, unable to speak. He gripped the windshield frame, craning his neck to get a better look at the dead creature. Finally, another breathy whisper trembled from his lips. "I… I never imagined…"

"You never imagined what?" Erin asked. When André didn't respond, she slammed a fist against the jeep's hood, trying to break him from his daze. "You know what's lying in that gunk back there?" she said. "What's left of my friend's nine-year-old daughter."

"It's not my fault."

"You knew," said Max.

"No…"

"Don't lie to me. You knew and didn't say anything."

"*Oui*. I suspected *something* was out there. A wild boar maybe. Or some big predator someone had abandoned on the island. But I had no idea it was something like this." André gazed again towards the monstrosity. "How can it be real?"

"Had its guts glopped all over me," Erin said. "It's fucking real alright."

Max stepped closer to the jeep, fixing a hard gaze on the Frenchman. "And it's not the only one."

"What? *Que dis-tu?*

"There's more," said Erin. "Much smaller than this one, but vicious."

André barely listened. He was too busy gazing at the massive centipede, transfixed by the sight of it. The gulls perched on its back were pecking at the insect now, probing the joints of its armored hide. "Those birds," said the Frenchman. "We need to stop them."

"Are you listening to us?" said Max. "We said…"

André cut him off with a shout. He slammed the steering wheel, blasting the jeep's horn to scare the birds off. "Get out of there! *Allez, dégage!*"

Erin scowled at him. "Why the fuck do you care?"

André kept hold of the windshield frame and glared down his nose at her. "Don't you understand? There is nothing like it in all the world. A rare commodity like that surely has value beyond measure."

Max held the rifle muzzle down, trying to make himself look less threatening. "But it isn't the only one. That's what we're trying to tell you. We think this thing had babies."

"We found tracks in the sand," Erin said. "Why don't you get out of the jeep and see for yourself."

"No. No. That won't be necessary. I believe you." Slowly, André sank back down into the driver's seat. The jeep's engine growled to life again.

"What are you doing?" Max's voice was a flatline—cold and serious.

"I will… I will return to the resort and warn the other guests."

Max edged closer to the jeep. "No, you won't. You're looking for a way to save your own skin."

They locked stares. Max saw the Frenchman's eye twitch, and knew instantly the guy was going to rabbit. Max took two lunging steps, reaching for the jeep's door, but he wasn't quick enough. André frantically shifted into reverse and the 4x4 shot backwards, its rugged tires spitting out a wave of sand.

Max brought the empty rifle to his shoulder, shouting, "Cut the engine and step out!" Putting on his best Marine sergeant's voice. Either André knew he was bluffing or was too afraid to comply. The jeep dug a crescent moon in the dirt as it wheeled around. Then it sped off towards the resort road.

Max lowered the rifle with a sigh. Erin placed a hand on his shoulder and he felt some of the tension give way.

"Fucking bastard," she said. "Did you see how he reacted to those birds?"

Max nodded. "The scumbag is already figuring out a way to profit from all this. Probably means to auction the body off to the highest bidder."

"What are we going to do?"

Max walked back to where he left the torn backpack. He dug out the bullets and dropped them into the pocket of his cargo shorts.

"You feel up to a jog?" he asked her.

SIXTEEN

"Hello? I know you can hear me. Hello?"

Alexander crossed the courtyard, barely able to hear the woman. He had driven back to the resort at dangerous speeds, twice almost careering off the rough road. Now his pulse pounded in his ears, a throbbing drum beat inside his skull. He walked in a daze, his whole world thrown off its axis.

"Don't walk away from me, Frenchie."

The American woman's grating voice finally broke Alexander from his trance. He wanted to quicken his pace, pretending not to hear her at all. But that was impossible. The classless bitch was practically shouting at him. If he wished to escape, Alexander would have to break out into a full-on sprint for his office. What a ridiculous sight that would make, he in khaki slacks and his silk guayabera shirt running like a common laborer. No, that would surely create suspicion amongst the guests. And *suspicion* was something he could not afford. So Alexander pasted on his most fawning smile and turned around.

"And how can I be of service, *mademoiselle*?" He wondered if she could see the lingering fear in his eyes. How could he possibly deal with this annoyance after what he'd just seen?

The woman was short with a gym-tight body and a scowling face. One look and Alexander could tell this one was a real *casse couilles*—a "ball breaker" as the Americans say. The woman adjusted the straps of her sundress then lowered her sunglasses so she could scowl at him. "You see this?" she said, holding up the latest iPhone. "Fourteen hundred I spent on this phone, and now I can't even check my *insta*."

"And the universe weeps," Alexander said under his breath. He kept looking around, throwing nervous glances over his shoulder, as if one of those horrid things would appear at any moment.

"What'd you say?"

"Only that I am sorry for the inconvenience. You see, there has been a problem with our cell tower. But rest assured, our maintenance crews are taking care of it as we speak."

"I hope so. You know, I dished out over six grand to be here. Then you people tell me the hiking trails are closed. And now this." She shoved her phone in his face. "What's next? You gonna close the beach too?"

Alexander's eye twitched. He wanted to slap the woman, screaming that he had bigger problems to deal with than some spoiled cunt. Namely, a giant man-eating centipede. Instead, Alexander spoke calmly through the clenched teeth of his smile. "Again, *mademoiselle*, I humbly apologize. But I promise you, the beach will remain open. And I hope to make all this up to you with our world-famous sunset luau. You won't be disappointed."

"I better not be," the ball breaker said. But Alexander had already turned his back on her, making a beeline for his private office.

Once inside, he locked the door and took in a few deep breaths, trying to steady his nerves. French colonial décor adorned the office, complete with bamboo shades over the windows and an antique ceiling fan lazily spinning above him. Still, sweat rolled down Alexander's forehead and drenched his armpits. He mopped his brow with a handkerchief then scampered over to his desk. It was an enormous piece of furniture, with delicate designs etched into its ebony hardwood surface. Waiting on his desktop was a package.

The box must have come in on the last ferry with the rest of the mail. A shipping label confirmed that it had been sent to the resort's PO box in Papeete. There was no return address, but the Frenchman noticed the faint writing on the package's side. It was in Russian.

Merde.

Nearly 30 centimeters tall, the package looked heavy. Alexander found a thin knife in his desk and slit through the packing tape. What appeared to be a large jar waited inside, gift wrapped in elegant black paper and topped with a gold metallic bow. Hesitant, Alexander tore through the paper, discovering a glass container full of murky liquid and floating pink, fleshy nubs. The label was in Russian too, but Alexander did not need to read it to know what he was looking at. Pigs' feet.

A card attached to the jar read, "You are in our thoughts, always." It was signed, *Sergei Popov.*

It took the Frenchman less than five seconds to realize the implication of the gift. His Russian oligarch investors owned, among other things, numerous pig farms. Rumor had it, when a subordinate crossed or merely displeased the Popov family, they soon disappeared, never to be seen again.

Never to be seen again because they'd been fed to packs of flesh-hungry swine.

This was no gift. It was a threat.

More sweat dripped from Alexander's brow as he dug into his desk for his walkie-talkie. He stabbed at the scan button a few times until a voice called out through a burst of static.

"North dock."

"This is Mr. André, I need something." He hoped the employee on the other end couldn't hear the panic in his voice.

"Of course, sir. What can I do for you?"

"Get the fishing boat gassed up and ready."

"But sir. It's a little late for fishing. Maybe we should…"

Alexander cut him off. "I didn't ask your opinion. Gas it up now. I want to be able to leave in a moment's notice."

The Frenchman shut off his walkie-talkie and hunched over to unlock the bottom drawer of his desk. He found the pistol waiting there and slid it out. It was a Walther PPK, the same gun James Bond had carried in the movies. Alexander had chosen it because he believed it held an air of sophistication and roguish bravado reserved for the upper class. Now, having seen the enormous creature, the pistol looked small and pathetic.

A summer blazer hung off the desk chair. Alexander slipped the pistol into its right pocket, knowing the bullets weren't for the monster. They were for anyone foolish enough to try to stop Alexander's escape.

Especially that fucking bouncer.

***

"I feel ridiculous," she said.

Augie Barnes flashed that shy, sheepish grin of his. "Trust me, you don't *look* ridiculous." They lingered near the edge of the party, outside of the ring of tiki torches the resort had set up. A live band were on stage near the swimming pool, playing pop versions of classic island tunes to tables full of guests under a massive pergola. The singles all wore casual yet fashionable vacation wear. Lots of high-end Hawaiian shirts and tight flowery sarongs with a skimpy cocktail dress mixed in here or there for good measure. Augie felt a bit out of place in his shorts and t-shirt (the t-shirt sporting the Princeton logo which he'd bought from Walmart). But he was used to feeling out of place. The girl, however, definitely stood out among the dinner crowd.

"But everyone is dressed for a luau, and I'm stuck with this." Her name was Malinda something and she gestured to herself with practiced rich-girl disgust. The outfit in question consisted of gray yoga pants that hugged the curve of her ass like a second skin and a matching top that clung so very tightly to her ample chest.

A cool ocean breeze swept through the pool area. Augie had a difficult time keeping his eyes off her nipples which strained against the skintight fabric. He wiped his thick glasses on the hem of his shirt, thinking whoever invented that Lycra material deserved a goddamn medal. Sure, her blonde hair was a bit of a tousled mess (she hadn't gotten to style it since morning yoga). But who cared? To Augie, it looked sexy as hell. How come bedhead looked saucy on women but made guys look like goofy-ass dorks?

"Maybe they'll open the road to the bungalows soon," said Augie. "You might be able to change right before they serve dinner."

Malinda was on the south side of thirty but she kicked at a pile of sand like a spoiled child. "What's taking them so fucking long? It's been closed all day. And the sun's going down."

"Well, Mr. André said they were fixing some sort of propane leak. He wants to make sure it's completely safe."

"It wouldn't be so bad," she said, pouting, "if they had their gift shops open. But it's empty and closed up tight. In fact, the whole resort is a ghost town. It's like half their help went on break at the same time."

Augie knew what she meant. Other than the party servers and the band, he'd barely seen an employee at the resort itself. Most of them were stationed on the edge of the hiking paths, almost like they were standing guard. Almost like they weren't going to let any of the guests leave.

But that was crazy thinking. That André bro was just being over protective. Augie couldn't even imagine the lawsuit that would drop if one of this crowd got hurt because of a gas leak.

"I just can't do it." Malinda crossed her arms, depriving Augie of his view. "I can't eat with everybody dressed like *this*. It's too embarrassing."

Augie had just met Malinda what's-her-name this morning. She was the head of HR at a big software firm with money to burn. A professional smoke show like her would've never given Augie Barnes "trust fund manchild" a second glance. But she sure seemed to be into Augie Barnes "Fortune 500 financial analyst." The decision to mock up all those fake social media profiles—making him look like hot shit—was turning out to be an awesome idea. He had another lady on the line—Tiffany he thought her name was. But she had disappeared after yoga. That was okay with Augie. Malinda's face wasn't quite as pretty, but *dammmmn* those tits of hers.

"Come on. I've got an idea." He led her up the grassy berm that separated the resort from the shoreline. When they reached the berm's peak, he spotted what he was looking for. "See that private cabana over there?"

She stood up tall on her tippy toes, searching the beach below. "Where?"

"Just down the shoreline a bit." It was a cute tent-like structure with a thatched roof and linen curtains for walls. You could keep the curtains open for a scenic ocean view. Or, better yet, you could close them for privacy. "How about you go make yourself comfortable in there, while I procure us some cocktails? Then I'll have the servers bring us a nice little dinner for two."

Malinda from HR gave Augie a sly smile he bet she never showed at the office. "Sounds perfect." She kissed his forehead then did a catwalk-worthy strut in the direction of the cabana, giving Augie another view of that yoga ass.

Neither of them heard the rattling hisses over the sounds of island music and crashing waves. Neither of them saw the two-foot-long insectile killers slithering across the beach with hungry, machine-like precision.

SEVENTEEN

His Converse were made for pavement, not a rough jungle path. So, as he crashed through the foliage, Max felt every rock and fallen tree branch right through the soles. He hadn't run holding a rifle like this since the Marines, and the muscles in his shoulders and chest burned. Erin dashed a few paces ahead of him. They'd been at it for maybe five minutes, moving at a good clip in and out of pools of shadow created by the high canopy. If the path had drawn a straight line to the resort, it'd be a little over three klicks long. But, instead, the trail weaved its way across the island snake-like through stands of trees and up rugged hills. Max didn't know how many kilometers it covered, but it was damn sure more than three. Erin had increased her pace as they went, a frantic intensity taking hold of her.

"Hey, hold up," Max called out to her. The bullets jingled in his pocket like spare change.

She stopped, hands on the curve of her hips, taking in deep breaths. "What's the matter, Marine? Can't keep up?" She might've meant to be playful, but there was no humor in her voice. After what they had seen, that wasn't a surprise.

"Probably not," Max said, breathing hard. "Too much beer and pizza lately. But that's not the point. We should conserve our energy. I know you want to warn the guests, but we don't know what we're running into."

Erin nodded. "Yeah, okay. Makes sense."

Max sucked in a few more breaths, his nose involuntarily crinkling up. He'd washed the bug guts from his skin, and must've accidentally rinsed off the hand sanitizer smeared under his nose. Now, the rotten seafood smell clung to him like a reeking cloud. It even overpowered the wet, earthy scents of the jungle around him.

He forced himself to ignore the stench and pushed on, keeping up a quick march. "Never got a chance to thank you."

"For what?" Erin glanced at him over her shoulder.

"If you hadn't gutted that giant freak with your spear, it would've made a quick snack out of me."

Even in dying sunlight, he could see her smile. Sweat glistened on her pale cheeks. "Where do you think that thing came from?"

"Haven't had much time to think on it, what with all the running and screaming and bug guts."

"You've got time now, cowboy. What are these freaks?"

Max glanced down at his sneaker, gathering his thoughts. "There was a species of prehistoric millipede around 300 million years ago. Only grew to be about nine feet long, but maybe it's related. It could've gone into some sort of hibernation and then…"

"I'm going to stop you right there." A hint of a smirk formed on her lips. "Remember when I said that unemployed historian line was a real panty dropper? Well, I just pulled the panties back up."

"Ok, that's unnecessarily mean. Let's hear your explanation, college girl."

"Aliens."

That stopped Max in his tracks. "I'm sorry, did you just say aliens?"

"I watched this video once suggesting life on earth originated on some distant planet. Bacteria or something rode here on a meteor. Maybe our freak did the same."

"I'd call that far-fetched."

"Yeah? What'd you call a fifty-foot-long, man-eating centipede?"

"Fair point."

They marched on in silence. The sun had sunk further but the breeze was still warm on their skin. Sweat dripped from Max's chin and drenched the pits of his shirt. "You want to hear another theory?"

"Hit me."

"From the 1960s to the '90s, France conducted nuclear tests in these waters. Thousands claimed to have gotten sick because of the fallout."

"Jesus, are you saying what I think you're saying?"

"What if those old sci-fi movies were right about nuclear radiation? You know, the ones with the giant ants and tarantulas and shit. What if the radiation somehow mutated the centipede population? They've had thirty years to evolve since then."

"They were living underground," she said, a faraway look in her eyes. "Then the construction crew showed up and began working on an expansion."

"Those crews need to dig some pretty deep holes," said Max. "Laying a foundation. Plumbing. Shit like that. Maybe they unearthed some sort of bug nest."

Erin shook her head, her eyes wide with disbelief. "Waking up this morning, I never imagined having a conversation about giant mutant insects. I can't believe…"

Max held a finger to his lips to cut the conversation short. He stood very still in the center of the path, holding the rifle at the ready.

Erin let several seconds of time pass before whispering, "What is it?"

"Listen," Max said.

The birds, normally yammering in the trees, had gone silent. "I don't hear any…"

Erin froze, her fair skin going pale white. One look at her face and Max could tell she heard it too—the long, rattling hiss, as alien a noise as anything Max had ever encountered. The sound of it was much softer than the hiss he'd heard before, but he could tell it was close.

Bringing the Remington to his shoulder, Max followed the noise. It led him to a wide stretch of the path bordered by thick bushes with wide green leaves.

Max could feel Erin sidle up behind him, close but not so close to restrict his movements. He used the rifle's barrel to part the big leaves. A horror show greeted him.

The thing that had collapsed in the bushes had once been a resort employee. Now it was nothing more than a bloody mass of ragged meat wrapped in torn, ragged fabric. Max thought it'd been a man, but couldn't be sure. Three of the baby freaks swarmed the corpse, their mandibles ripping flesh right off the bone. The bugs had eaten so much already, they resembled blood-fattened ticks. Their bodies were bloated and engorged, yet they kept on eating. Fixated on their feast, the creatures didn't seem to notice Max's existence.

Behind him, Erin did her best to stifle the gasp, but Max could still hear the breath catch in her throat. Keeping his rifle up and trained on the freaks, he jutted his chin, gesturing to a large rock by the side of the path. Without uttering a word, Erin bent down to pick it up.

"On the count of three," Max whispered. "One…"

He took aim. He would've liked to step back a dozen feet and shoot from a distance, but then the brush would fall back into place, obscuring his shot. So it had to be up close and personal.

"Two…" Max whispered.

He slipped his finger inside the trigger guard. Beside him, Erin hefted the big rock above her head, ready to bring it crushing down.

"Three!"

***

Malinda strolled across the beach towards the cabana, listening to the tacky island band playing in the distance. Malinda was okay with missing the pool-side luau. She had a much more interesting party in mind with the rich simp she'd snagged.

She kept her back to him, knowing Augie's eyes were locked on her body with every step she took. Slipping into the cabana, she waited a few beats before finally turning around.

"So predictable," she whispered to herself.

Augie, the poor little lamb, practically sprinted back to the pool bar. Smiling to herself, Malinda felt like every bit the seductive vampire as she untied the cabana's curtains. Once the curtains were drawn, a little lamp came alive inside, giving the place a soft romantic glow. The resort knew what they were doing. And so did Malinda.

She had told the financial wunderkind she was head of HR at her firm. Truth was, she'd just started the job there, and she fucking hated it. She'd lied about renting a bungalow too. Malinda nearly maxed out her credit card just to afford the smallest room in the resort's main building. But she knew how good she looked in her yoga pants and wanted an excuse to stay in them all day. She also wanted an excuse to get him alone. Thank God for the path closure.

Deftly, she shimmied out of her top then sat on a chaise lounge to roll off her yoga pants. They were so tight, it felt like shedding a second skin. She wore no bra, no panties, and stood completely nude in the lamp's glow. A complementary bottle of coconut-scented sunscreen sat on a table beside the chaise. Malinda quickly squirted a glob into her hands to lather herself up. She'd been sweating in the tropical heat all day and didn't want a whiff of B.O. to ruin her plans.

She could clearly hear the band playing for the luau crowd. Island pop tunes weren't exactly ideal, but once Augie got a look at her, Malinda doubted he'd even notice the music. Sprawling out on the chaise, she pulled a beach towel over her firm naked body. She wanted to watch Augie's expression as she revealed herself to him. Of course, Malinda had no intention of having sex with the guy. Oh, she'd let him do stuff to her. And she might even do a few things for him. But actual intercourse was off the table, for now. No way was Malinda giving that up for free.

No, Malinda planned to leave him wanting more. And more. And more. She was working the long game and intended to get everything she could from poor Augie—jewelry, European vacations, a rent-free love nest. If she played it right, she might even get a ring out of him—without a prenup, of course.

Malinda settled back against the chaise and closed her eyes. She would keep her eyes shut later and fantasize about Chris Evans while Augie did his thing. Maybe she would…

Malinda's eyes snapped open. A soft rattling sound echoed through the cabana.

What was that?

Holding the towel against her body, Malinda sat up and scanned the cabana. She squinted in the dim light, no longer appreciating the cabana's romantic mood lighting.

There's nothing here, she thought to herself. Then she heard the hiss again, louder this time. She quickly jerked her feet up to the chaise, like a kid playing *the floor is lava.*

Actually, the cabana had no flooring. Instead, it was built over a soft bed of white sand. Something under that sand was moving—like a little white wave circling around the cabana. The sand mound suddenly changed course and squirmed straight towards her. Malinda pushed herself back farther on the chaise, pulling the towel to her mouth. She bit down on the cloth to keep from screaming. The civilized part of her psyche refused to accept what she saw.

This can't be real. It can't be. It can't be.

A red and black blur burst out of the sandy floor and shot towards her. It took Malinda's brain a half-second to register the long, segmented insect body, the mandibles, the twitching antennae. It was two feet long with dozens of sharp legs that jabbed into her bare flesh like sewing machine needles. The thing bit her once on the inner thigh—a sharp burning that forced a scream from Malinda's lips. She instantly regretted it.

The mutant centipede cut Malinda's scream short by plunging into her wide-open mouth. Desperate, she grabbed the thing's tail end and yanked with all her strength. But it was no use. The creature only wiggled through her fingers, burrowing deeper down her throat. Malinda hacked and coughed, her gag reflex trying to dislodge the invader. She felt the needle legs puncture the soft tissue of her throat as the thing crawled deeper and deeper inside of her. Then she felt the mandibles bite down.

It's eating me! her brain was screaming. *Eating me from the inside!*

She thrashed on the chaise, tears streaming from her eyes, snot bubbling out of her nose. A mournful, muffled scream escaped from the deep recesses of her vocal cords.

Then the venom took effect.

EIGHTEEN

A split-second after Max shouted *three*, he squeezed the trigger. The Remington boomed. The mutant bug's head exploded with a sickening *SPLUUUT*, spraying white, puss-like slime in all directions.

Next to him, Erin let out a fierce yell and threw the stone with all her strength. Her intended target was gnawing on the dead employee's leg when the rock came down, crushing its long body against the ground. The thing thrashed and hissed, but it could not wiggle itself out from under the rock.

Abandoning its feast, the third centipede rushed at Max, baring mandibles dripping with human blood. No time to work the Remington's bolt, Max shuffled back several feet and hammered down with the butt of his rifle. The freak kept squirming, even though half its head was mush. So Max hit it again.

No reason to waste a bullet, thought the ex-marine.

Erin found a new stone and stalked towards the surviving creature, still squirming to get free. She raised the big rock high above her head and let gravity do the rest. The centipede's head burst like a rotten melon.

Max turned away. He didn't want to look at the ravaged corpse any longer than he had to. He'd seen his share of dead men in the war and never wanted to get used to the sight.

"What was he doing out here?"

Erin hugged herself, fighting back a sob. "That André asshole knew something was going on out here. I bet he sent employees to keep the guests off the paths."

He slid the rifle's bolt back to chamber another round. Then he bent low, inspecting the path. The dirt trail looked as if some lunatic had stabbed it thousands of times with a golf tee. But eyeing it closely, Max could discern dozens of separate tracks. They weaved around and crisscrossed each other wildly, but they were all leading in the same direction. "They're still heading for the resort."

Erin covered her mouth with her hand, taking in short breaths, regaining her composure. Max was surprised she kept her breakfast down. "Okay," she said. "Just give me a second and I'll be ready."

Max nodded grimly. "You know, it might be safer if you went back to the bungalows and hunkered down."

"What?" She caught her breath and squinted at him with those intense green eyes.

"I'm saying you don't need to go."

"I know what you're saying. I just can't believe it."

"Erin, I can handle this by myself."

"Not a chance, Marine," Erin said, some steel coming back to her voice. "In case you forgot, these things fucking ate my friend."

"I'm all too aware of that. And I don't want the same to happen to you."

She stabbed a finger hard into his chest. "So, I'm supposed to hide somewhere while these bugs chow down on the others? That's not me, Max. Besides, I'm not exactly helpless. It was me who gutted the big one, remember?"

"If I lived to be a thousand, I'd never forget that."

"Then it's settled." Erin marched down the path, not looking his way.

Max jogged to catch up. Even under the dire circumstances, Max felt a grin coming on. Where had this woman been all his life? More than anything, he wanted to know her better.

He hoped they both survived so he'd get the chance.

***

Alexander tried not to break into a run as he quick-walked from the hotel. He'd thrown on his summer blazer and could feel the weight of the pistol in the right pocket and the walkie-talkie in the left. A duffle bag hung off his shoulder, filled with the contents of his office safe—a few thousand dollars' worth of French Pacific Francs, some insurance contracts, and a $4,000 bottle of Macallan 30-year double cask scotch. After the events of today, Alexander would likely break open the Macallan on the boat and drink straight from the bottle.

The band his assistant had hired played poolside, filling the resort grounds with pleasing island tunes. Keeping his head down, Alexander ignored the trite music and circled around to the side of the hotel where his jeep awaited. Here, the partygoers couldn't see him. He took three strides towards it and stopped dead.

Lying face down on the gravel road, an older member of the maintenance staff trembled and thrashed. At first glance, Alexander thought the man was having a seizure. Then the Frenchman noticed the long, snake-like insect wrapped around the man's neck. Vastly bigger than a household centipede, the creature was a miniature version of the monstrous thing Alexander had seen out by the private bungalows. *A baby*, just like the redheaded bartender had said.

And now this *baby* was feasting on one of his employees, the old man making desperate gurgling noises. Blood bubbled out of his flesh and painted the gravel red.

Merde.

Hand trembling, Alexander slowly reached for a fallen shovel, no doubt dropped by his dying employee. The Frenchman thought about using the Walther PPK, but was afraid the island band wasn't loud enough to cover up a gunshot. So instead, Alexander edged close to the thrashing man and raised the shovel over his head, like a neanderthal's club. He swung as hard as he could, but the bag hanging from his shoulder threw off his aim. The shovel head had merely grazed the centipede and thudded against the gravel.

Mon Dieu!

Bile churned up André's throat. He let the shovel clang to the ground and shuffled back several feet. The centipede squirmed away from its victim as if drunk, then came to a sudden stop. Alexander didn't think he'd hit the freak hard enough to kill it, but he sure as hell stunned the bastard.

The Frenchman left his employee to die and scrambled to his jeep. He was about to start the engine when a wild thought flashed in his brain.

Back in his office, a jar of pigs' feet sat on his desk, a jar that could be emptied. A jar big enough to accommodate a mutant creature never before seen by mankind.

***

Augie waited a few beats, before hightailing it to the tiki bar. Too bad that hot redhead wasn't working tonight. He wouldn't mind getting another look at her. But what did it matter now? He had his sights on bigger game.

He ordered two margaritas with an extra shot of Patron in each (He'd found tequila to be a better lube than Astroglide). Then the trust fund manchild fast-walked over the berm and back to the cabana, careful not to spill a drop. His pulse rose a notch when he noticed that Malinda had closed the cabana's curtains.

"Hope you like margaritas." Augie swooped inside the tent, his shy grin replaced by a wolfish one.

The smile instantly vanished.

"Malinda?"

She was flat on her stomach, face down on the chaise lounge and completely naked. Seeing a woman like that would've normally given Augie an instant hard-on. But there was nothing seductive about Malinda's pose. She was stiff and her limbs were splayed out in unnatural positions. Worse yet, her body trembled weakly, like a toy running low on battery power. Augie inched towards her, a cold tremor working its way up his spine.

"Malinda, what's wrong?"

Now, he noticed the specks of blood splattered across the chaise's pillows. Maybe she was having a seizure and had bit her tongue. What was he supposed to do about that? Give aid or run for help? Since Augie didn't know fuck all about giving CPR, he decided to crash the luau and scream his lungs out for a doctor.

He was about to turn to dash through the cabana curtains when he heard the soft crunching. It reminded him of a time when he was a boy and his beloved beagle crawled under the house with a stolen chicken bone.

Augie didn't want to turn back, but a morbid curiosity compelled him to. Something in his brain wouldn't let him leave until he found out where the sound was coming from.

"Can you hear me?" He shook Malinda's bare shoulder, getting no response. The soft crunching sounds continued, emanating from somewhere inside her chest. "I... I'm going for help. Malinda?"

Gently, he pulled on her shoulder, rolling the woman onto her back. His heart stopped cold. Malinda stared up at him with wide lifeless eyes, her mouth twisted open into an obscene scream. The tail of some impossibly large insect hung out of her mouth, squirming. A horrible realization immediately struck him. The "crunching" noise was the sound of the creature feasting on Malinda's insides.

"Holy fuck."

Augie stumbled backwards, fumbling over his own flip-flops. He sat down hard on the cabana's sandy floor and tried to scramble to his feet. He made it to his hands and knees before something hard and sharp stabbed his calf. It was another one of those things. A two-foot-long centipede, wrapping itself around his leg. Its sharp legs latched onto Augie's flesh as its mandibles shot hot venom into his muscles.

A scream leapt from Augie's throat—the kind of scream he hadn't heard himself bellow since he was a small child. A high-pitched wail devoid of all ego or pride. Augie fell on his side and frantically tried to kick the centipede away. Then he felt more tiny daggers piercing the back of his neck. Without seeing it, he knew it was another freakish centipede, injecting him with its venom.

Screaming out again, Augie clawed himself up and crawled desperately for the cabana curtains. If he could just get outside, maybe someone from the party would see him. Augie knew it was his only hope.

He crawled until he could no longer feel his limbs, and his body crashed to the ground. Augie opened his mouth but a shout would no longer come. He reached out for the curtains with a trembling hand but they were beyond his grasp. The sounds of the party outside became warped and faint as if Augie was underwater. A poppy rendition of Bob Marley's "Get Up, Stand Up" was the last thing he heard before glancing down at his waist. Yet another centipede skittered up his thigh and burrowed underneath his shorts.

It began to eat.

Thanks to the venom surging through his veins, Augie couldn't physically react to the pain. But he could feel every second of it. He gnashed his teeth together so hard he thought they'd shatter. Then he prayed for a death that wouldn't come quickly enough.

NINETEEN

The trees along the path became shorter and shorter, the undergrowth more manicured. Max could see the path now, winding towards the resort in the distance, caught in the sunset's warm glow. He and Erin slowed their pace—listening, watching. To the right, a high, grassy ridge blocked their view of the west beach. The surging tide's cadence mixed with faint music that drifted towards them from the resort's pool area.

As they marched on, Max dug the loose ammo out of his pocket. He counted nine spare rounds, three left in the rifle's magazine, and one chambered and ready to go.

"How many you got there?" Erin asked.

"Thirteen in all."

"That's not enough, is it?"

Max thought about the tracks he'd seen, countless feet crisscrossing each other, and shook his head.

They heard the chaos before they saw it. Heart-stopping shrieks pierced the darkening night. Louder than the crashing surf or the music that abruptly cut out. There was an ancient fear in those screams—a long forgotten fear that was still hardwired deep in the psyche. The fear of being prey.

They dashed around the tennis courts, and Max heard Erin gasp beside him. A hundred yards away, people scrambled desperately away from the pool area. Most were guests—men in their tacky Hawaiian shirts, women in their tropical sarongs. They ran for their lives, heading for the main hotel building. The contrast between the guest's festive attire and their bloodcurdling screams was obscenely comical. But Max wasn't laughing. Not after he saw what was behind them.

"Sweet Jesus," Erin murmured, her words a whispered prayer. "So many of them."

The monstrosity's babies swarmed the edge of the resort—dozens of them, maybe hundreds. Thousands of scurrying legs rubbed together creating a cacophony of terrifying hisses.

At the edge of the pool deck, a dark-haired woman stumbled to the manicured lawn and the centipedes were instantly on her. Max brought the gun up and took quick aim. He swallowed a curse. There was nothing he could do for her. She thrashed in the grass then succumbed to their flesh-ripping mandibles. Max wanted to kill the bastards for what they'd done. But the ex-marine knew he needed to save his bullets for immediate threats. These ones were too busy with their feast to attack anyone else.

Max swept the rifle to the right and found a new target—a single centipede about three feet long racing behind a chubby guy in his thirties. Max tried leading the bug, but it was so quick, so snake-like in its movements, it was hard to track. His shot missed by nearly a foot. Max worked the bolt and fired again. Once more, his shot went wide.

"Shit." He hissed the word through clenched teeth as he chambered another round. He let out a long breath, trying to steady his nerves, and pulled the trigger. The Remington barked and the creature's head disintegrated into a bursting cloud of goo. Max racked the bolt back and fired again, killing a second bug about to take down a tall bird-like woman with a platinum blonde ponytail.

Nine bullets left.

Lowering the rifle, Max realized a horrible truth. The centipede's hunger was all-consuming, undeterred by fear or self-preservation. Their appetite for human flesh was so insatiable, not even the crack of his gunshots could scare them away.

"The hotel!" Erin screamed beside him. She was shouting at the guests, frantically urging them towards the main building. "Get to the hotel!"

Max reloaded and fired three more rounds, taking his time with each shot. He didn't have the luxury to miss. Three more freaks died, their insectile heads popping like overgrown zits. At the sound of his gunshots, one poor guest instinctively dove to the ground for cover. The guy paid with his life. A centipede raced up his back and went for his neck. A mandible slit his carotid artery and blood geysered up, spraying the guests that ran past his jerking body.

Poor bastard.

A band had set up on the pool deck stage—burly islanders in matching print shirts and traditional sarongs. The bass player swung his instrument like a battle axe, batting away one centipede after another, until a freak spiraled around his leg and disappeared up his man-skirt. The islander dropped his bass to grab his crotch, but it was too late to save himself. The burly man screeched and four more centipedes snaked around his body before he even had a chance to fall. The lead guitarist died moments later after he stumbled over the drum kit trying to run away. Cymbals clanged and clashed against the pool deck as the centipedes swarmed him.

More guests surged towards Max and Erin like a herd of spooked cows. Some screamed. Others just ran with panicked breath. Max couldn't get a shot off through them, so he found himself shoving his way in the opposite direction. Next to him, Erin kept shouting, "Everyone in the hotel! Everyone inside!"

Twenty yards behind them, a jeep bounded onto the dirt road, its engine a low growl. Max risked a glance at it and spotted André behind the wheel, all alone. A few black-shirted employees poured into the road, trying to wave him down. They no doubt saw the jeep as a means of escape. The jeep's horn let out a long wail. When the crowd didn't disperse, the vehicle plowed through them, knocking their bodies aside as if they were children's toys.

"Motherfucker." Max felt the urge to bring the rifle up but knew he couldn't spare the bullet.

The jeep careened off the road then skidded in reverse. A tall islander who had survived a ride on its grill now rushed the vehicle, clawing at its door. Max never saw André bring up the pistol, but heard the familiar pops of small caliber gunfire. A moment later, the man was down on the road.

Spitting gravel, the jeep slid backwards several feet. Then it shot forward, rumbling down the road at dangerous speeds, disappearing behind a thick stand of trees.

Max felt as if a lead weight was crushing against his chest. He couldn't bare the thought of that rich fuck getting away. But there was nothing he could do. He turned back to the resort and spotted several figures sprinting across his field of vision, running for the tree line.

They've lost it, he thought. The jungle was the centipede's domain. They would never outrun them in there.

"No," Max shouted. "Over here!"

Erin joined him, shouting her voice hoarse. Either the guests didn't hear them or fear had consumed all reason. Max couldn't see the creatures that chased them—the freaks hidden by tall grass. But he knew they were there.

None of the vacationers even made it to the tree line. One by one, the runners fell and their screams echoed across the resort grounds.

The rest of the beach crowd crashed through the hotel doors. Two centipedes slipped inside behind them before the doors slammed shut. Max hoped the guests would band together and stomp the bastards into goo.

The ex-marine didn't have the luxury to think about them right now. He had other problems. Like the two bleach-blondes who'd trapped themselves in the pavilion cantina. The young ladies shrieked bloody murder as they hiked up their party dresses to clamor up onto a table, as if the centipedes couldn't climb up after them. A pack of freaks emerged from the grassy berm and skittered towards the pavilion, seeking fresh kills.

"Come on," Erin shouted as she broke into a sprint. "We've got skanks to save."

Max almost snorted out a laugh as he took off after her.

TWENTY

Did I just kill a man?

Alexander white-knuckled the steering wheel as the jeep thundered along the path, headlights cutting blades of light in the dark jungle. His mind should have been on the road in front of him, but all Alexander thought about was that damned employee who had tried to yank open the driver-side door. One moment the lanky islander was standing there outside his window, snarling curses at him. Then the man was suddenly lying in the roadway. Alexander didn't remember pulling the pistol, much less firing it. It all happened so quickly.

The gun sat on the passenger seat now, next to the big jar with the mutant centipede scrambling around inside. Alexander glanced down at it, wondering how that little chunk of metal would transform his life. When he looked back at the dark road, a curse hissed through his clenched teeth.

Merde!

In retrospect, Alexander should have just run over the man. He was surely already dead. But the sight of him lying there, his bloody corpse swarming with centipedes, startled the Frenchman. Instinctively, Alexander jerked hard on the wheel, but was too slow, and the driver-side tires thudded over the corpse. The jeep careened wildly off the road and skidded into a ditch.

No! No! No! Alexander shifted into reverse and pressed his full weight on the accelerator. But the wheels only whirled freely in mid-air, finding no road to grip on to. Alexander shifted into drive and stomped on the gas pedal again. No luck.

That is when Alexander noticed both his pistol and the jar were missing. The abrupt drop into the ditch must have thrown both to the floorboards.

What if the glass broke? What if that thing is free?

The Frenchman's heart raced as he clawed at his seatbelt. A moment later, he spotted the jar, fully intact, and allowed himself a sigh of relief. The two-foot centipede skittered inside, angry but still imprisoned. Alexander collected the jar, his pistol, and the duffle bag then dropped out of the jeep into the ditch. Deck shoes slipping, Alexander scrambled out of the little ravine and up onto the road. The whole time, he kept his eyes on the corpse.

Was it Nathan or Jonathan? Alexander was not very good with names. But he knew the poor bastard was a resort employee, the man's polo shirt giving him away. The creatures did not appear to be bothered by the incident with the jeep. They had returned to the dead man and gnawed away at his ribcage… his belly… his fingers and toes.

Crunch. Crunch. Crunch.

Vomit rose up in Alexander's throat. He swallowed it down and ran headlong into the dark jungle, making a desperate dash for the north docks. Blood throbbed through his veins, pounding in his ears. Maybe if he kept moving, the freaks wouldn't catch him. Maybe…

If he hadn't been so terrified, Alexander may have noticed the distant hissing sound racing through the jungle like a runaway freight train rattling on its tracks.

***

"What booze is the most flammable?" Max frantically rummaged through the bottles behind the pool-side bar. The rifle lay on the bar top, within quick reach.

Erin gave him a sideways glance. "What are you talking about?" She clutched a goo-splattered table leg, her chest rising and falling rapidly as she tried to catch her breath. The bleach-blonde guests huddled behind her. The ladies trembled like rain-soaked poodles, no doubt in shock.

"Oh my fucking God," one said over and over. "Oh my fucking God." The other bit her quivering lip and stayed quiet.

Max couldn't blame them. Two minutes earlier, he and Erin had rushed to the pool's pavilion and promptly shot, stomped, and bashed four more of the demonic 100-legged bastards. The whole time, the female guests (aka the "skanks") stayed on the table top, hugging each other as they screamed their lungs out. By all appearances, Max and Erin had cleared the pool area of the insect freaks. Still, it took some coaxing to get the ladies down from their perch.

Now, Max was behind the bar, eyeing the label on a bottle. The gunshots and terrified screams still rang in his ears, so he found himself shouting. "How about tequila?"

"Not really a time for margaritas, Marine." Erin pointed her stained table leg at the hotel's main building. "We've got plenty more bugs surrounding the hotel. It's only a matter of time before they get inside."

"That's why I'm asking which alcohol is the most flammable."

Realization must have hit because Erin dropped her club and slipped down behind the bar. When she popped back up, she gripped a couple of bottles in each hand. "Tequila is okay. But overproof rum and Sambuca would work better. Especially when we mix it with this."

Erin reached below the bar again and brought out a metal container of lighter fluid, probably used to ignite the tiki torches.

Max nodded then looked to the frightened ladies. "I know you're scared, but I need you to rip up some bar rags into strips. Make sure they're dry. Can you do that for me?"

Before the ladies could answer, Max darted back to the banquet area and found two tiki torches still flickering. He ripped them from the ground and returned to the bar. A dead centipede crunched under his sneaker, spurting viscous goo across the floor.

Erin had already lined up several bottles and was prying off the metal pour spouts. The bleach-blondes were cutting strips from a bar towel with some lime knives they had found. Their hands shook, but having an activity calmed their nerves some.

Max threw a glance at the hotel. The ground was alive with dozens of the mutant centipedes, squirming around the front entrance. A few had begun to crawl up the face of the building, antennae twitching, feeling for an entrance. The freaks could sense there were plenty of survivors to feast on, if they could only find a way inside.

Those climbers would be a problem. Max had used two more bullets saving the blondes. That left only four shots to take out those fuckers before they slipped in through an open window.

Erin stepped up behind Max and followed his gaze to the hotel. "We better get over there."

Max glanced at the bar top, seeing the booze bombs were ready to go. Strips of towels hung from the bottlenecks, dripping with lighter fluid. He handed the tiki torches to the guests then slung the rifle over his shoulder and grabbed as many bottles as he could carry.

"Stay close and try not to scream in my ear," he told the blondes.

The one who'd been chanting "Oh my fucking God" shook her head. She was hugging the tiki torch like a security blanket. "I… I don't know if I can."

The other pleaded with her wide, wet, racoon eyes. All the tears hadn't done her mascara any favors. "Can't we just stay back here where it's safe?"

"Nowhere is safe." Erin's voice was flat and cold.

"It's your choice," said Max. "But if more of those fuckers sneak up on you, we won't be around."

"You probably stand a better chance sticking with us," said Erin.

The ladies shared a silent look. Then, as if telepathically linked, they turned in unison to face Max and Erin. "We'll do whatever you say."

"Good," said Max. "Start by bringing that fire over here."

He held an Italian bottle of Sambuca up to a tiki torch and lit the fuse.

Here goes fucking nothing.

TWENTY-ONE

Kreessssh!

The first bottle smashed against the concrete pathway a few yards from the hotel. Liquid fire spewed among a tangle of writhing centipedes. It may not have been a traditional Molotov cocktail, filled with gasoline, but it still scorched the mutant bastards. Besides, a gasoline fire might spread to the hotel. The flaming Sambuca only burned the bugs. They squirmed wildly, hissing as their hard exoskeletons lit up like bananas foster.

Cheers erupted from inside the hotel. Survivors huddled by the lobby windows, watching the action. Max wished they'd spend their time barricading the place instead.

Beside him, Erin tossed another bottle, frying more of the freaks. In their agony they tried to crawl away while flames rose from their shells. The bodily fluids inside their exoskeletons began to boil and pressure built up. Their bodies burst like popcorn, vomiting goo in all directions.

Max didn't have time to watch the carnage. He brought up the Remington and took aim. The sun had gone down, but luckily a full moon was rising and plenty of exterior lights illuminated the hotel. Max put a crawler in his sights, a centipede close to a third-story window. The rifle barked. The mutant fell, leaving its brains behind, a splattered pus stain on the hotel's façade.

Max missed with his next shot, cursing under his breath. Quickly, he worked the bolt and fired again. Another freak fell from the building and crunched to the sidewalk below. Before Max could chamber another round, the last of the climbers found an open window on the fourth floor and skittered inside.

Fuck. The guests inside would have to take care of that one.

With one bullet left, Max slung his rifle and grabbed another booze bomb. Erin had done good work. Flaming bugs littered the hotel's front lawn. A strange bitter smell rose from their corpses—like the scent of moths being fried by a bug zapper. Too bad the surviving creatures didn't turn tail and run. Instead, they scurried straight towards Max and the ladies. Whatever notions of "fear" hardwired into their bug brains were overridden by insatiable insect hunger.

"Fall back," Max shouted as he tossed a bottle underhand. It shattered, creating a short wall of flame in front of the encroaching bugs. The centipedes crawled right through the blaze, most of them moving so quickly their shells didn't catch on fire. The last three weren't so fortunate. They hissed and twitched as the flames took them.

Erin's bottle sailed through the air in a high arc, but hit grass instead of concrete and didn't shatter.

There were two bottles of rum left. Max and Erin each gripped one. They shot each other desperate glances.

"Light the fuses, then run," Max told the blondes. The ladies did as instructed, then dashed back towards the pool. With flaming tikis in hand, they looked like Olympic torch bearers—if the bearers wore slinky dresses and ran like clumsy third-graders.

Max took the time to grin. Then he spotted centipedes closing in.

"Same time," he said to Erin.

She nodded. "Don't you miss, cowboy."

They threw together, underhand soft-ball pitches. The bottles tumbled through the air, end over end. This time, both hit the concrete path, splashing flaming rum in all directions, lighting up the night. It spread like napalm among the mutant bugs. Their hisses died in a burst of crackling flames.

A guttural roar filled Max's ears, and he realized that it was him, screaming a war cry. Erin joined in and they bellowed together as they watched the burning centipedes pop in the night.

There were a few survivors. Finally, their preservation instincts had kicked in, overruling their appetite, and they slinked off towards the dark jungle path. Max thought maybe he should hunt them down and finish this. But he was too damn exhausted and didn't want to risk fighting these freaks in the dark. Better to check the survivors in the hotel and help with any wounded.

Erin slumped down and sat on the grass. Her nose crinkled against the stench of burning bugs. "Who's going to believe this?"

"We've got plenty of evidence." Max gestured towards the burning bug corpses scattered across the resort grounds. "And a hotel full of witnesses."

"Not full anymore," said Erin, her voice cracking. "Wish we could've saved them."

"We did all we could." Max sat down next to her.

"It wasn't enough."

"It never is. But there's people who will see tomorrow because of what you did today. You handled yourself like a true badass. Would've made one hell of a marine."

She grinned at him. "I do look good in green."

A pulsating soreness worked its way into his muscles. Max ignored it and struggled to his feet. He offered Erin his hand. "Come on. We should check on the others. A few of those things got inside the building."

"No rest for the wicked." Erin sighed and let him hoist her up to her feet. "When all this is over, you're taking me on a proper date."

"By *proper* do you mean pizza or burgers?"

She shook her head. "No sir. I'm talking white tablecloths and a wine list."

Max snorted. He was about to respond when a terrible hiss echoed across the resort grounds, the sound of it sending icy spikes up his spine.

"No," said Erin, shaking her head. "It can't be. We killed it."

Max held a finger to his lips, cutting her off so he could pinpoint the sound. He gazed at the dark jungle path more than 100 yards away. Branches shook. Trees swayed to one side. Something was moving around among all the dark foliage. Something big.

It was so damn obvious. Max cursed himself for missing it. Some dusty corner of his brain remembered a nugget of information from his youth. It came from one of those sensationalistic nature books for kids—the gruesome detail that, upon hatching, *some* baby centipedes devour their mothers. Maybe Max had been counting on that possibility. More than likely, he was so focused on their immediate survival he somehow forgot the most basic of facts.

It takes two to make babies.

A second mega centipede burst from the jungle. Its glossy red and black exoskeleton gleamed in the moonlight. It was bigger than the one Erin had gutted at the bungalows. Max knew female insects were often larger than the males. But if this thing was a mom, it certainly didn't show any maternal affection. When the baby freaks tried to slither past it, the creature snatched them up with its huge mandibles and slurped them into its pulsating mouth like they were spaghetti noodles.

In unison, the blondes let loose with deafening shrieks. One of them sprinted for the beach, trying to get as much distance between her and that monstrosity as she could. The other made a dash for the hotel, no doubt thinking she would be safer inside. It was a fatal mistake.

She made it ten yards before the monstrous centipede sensed her movements. With machine-like precision, it raced to intercept her, its multitude of enormous legs punching perfect holes in the resort lawn. The creature swooped down and impaled the screaming woman with its mandibles. The blonde arched her back, letting out a last anguished cry—a final rejection of a cruel and merciless world. But the cry fell on pitiless ears. The creature kept its grip until the venom took hold, then shoved the woman into its mouth. The blonde's scream died instantly. It was an obscene kindness that the creature devoured her head first.

Horrified, Max watched the mutant's skull wobble up and down as it crunched through flesh and bone. Erin stood frozen beside him. She brought a hand to her lips to keep from screaming. She nearly lost it when blood gushed from the freak's mouth followed by spurts of hanging entrails.

It took the monster only seconds to finish its meal. Then it turned towards the hotel, its antennae twitching. Like its babies, the creature could somehow sense the humans darting around inside. And it wanted them.

Max remembered the other mega freak crashing through the bungalow like it was made of popsicle sticks. He didn't have much hope the hotel would keep the thing out.

"Erin, you with me?" He didn't move a muscle and kept his words to a whisper.

"Yeah, I'm here." Her voice gave her away. She was nearly broken. Nearly, but not completely. There was still an ounce of steel left in her tone. Max hoped it would be enough.

"Do we have any of those bombs left?" he asked.

TWENTY-TWO

He was a fucking mess. Alexander lost count of how many times he had stumbled along the dark jungle trail. Branches had lashed at his face and thorns had clawed at his arms. Dirt smeared his summer blazer and blood dribbled from a dozen tiny cuts. Yet through it all, he hugged the big jar tight to his body, keeping the glass intact.

"Merci à Dieu," he whispered to himself, even though the Frenchman knew God had nothing to do with tonight's events.

Out of breath, Alexander pressed forward until he could see the dock lights in the distance. He broke free from the jungle and allowed himself a slower pace across the wild grass path to the harbor. He sucked in gulps of air, trying to slow his racing heart.

At this time of night, at least two employees worked at the docks. They should be down there now, cleaning and prepping the boats. But Alexander saw no one and heard no chatter. A now familiar fear began to creep into the primitive recesses of his brain. Alexander sensed something was very wrong here.

He came to a dead stop along the path and crouched low to the dirt. It was a stupid thing to do. Making himself small and still might hide him from a man, but it would do nothing to conceal him from these… *things*. Still, he kept low and did not move—guided by some instinct far older than reason.

Slowly he reached into the blazer's pocket and dug out his walkie-talkie. "*Allooo*, north dock?" Alexander whispered.

He was answered by nothing but static.

"This is Mr. André. Is there anyone there?"

Again, there was no answer.

For several minutes, Alexander did not move. He crouched in the moonlight among the tall grass and simply listened. There was nothing to be heard but the breeze sweeping across the shoreline and the lap of waves against the dock posts. Eventually, he willed himself to stand and walk to the harbor.

What he saw there set his heart racing once more. A slick of red gore was splattered across the boardwalk. It was a grisly stew with strips of torn flesh and shards of bone floating in the blood. The remnants of a meal.

The little ones would have left more than this.

Images flashed in Alexander's brain. He remembered the massive centipede sprawled out near the bungalows, dead but still terrifying. Its armored insectile shell gleamed in the sunshine. Its long legs appeared as cruel and sharp as spears. Its nightmarish mandibles dripped with gore.

A stark and sudden terror welled up inside of Alexander, and he ran headlong down the docks. His deck shoes slipped in the gore and left bloody footprints all the way to the boat.

***

A chorus of screams erupted from the hotel. The guests inside were powerless. They could do nothing but watch in horror as the mega centipede slithered in a sidewinder motion, building up momentum. Hissing, the creature bulleted straight towards the hotel and crashed against its façade. The whole building shook. The thick entryway doors exploded into splinters and deep cracks broke out across the brickwork. A few more slams like that and the thing would have a hole big enough to slither inside.

Max watched the scene play out as he crept across the resort grounds towards the creature's backside. He was alone. Erin hid in the poolside pavilion, waiting in the darkness. He wished she would be safe back there, but he knew the truth. As long as this thing was still kicking, no one was safe.

Three booze bombs trembled in Max's grasp. He winced, hearing the *clink, clink, clink* of the bottles with every step. *Could the freak hear it too?*

When Max fought the smaller ones, he'd gotten to a place beyond fear. It was the same back in Afghanistan. In the day-to-day quiet moments, a creeping dread could overtake you. But in the thick of a firefight, there was no time to be scared. You put your head down and did your job.

Max wished he could get to that place now. In the face of this *thing*—this primordial monstrosity beyond reason—he fought to keep himself from running in the opposite direction.

"How the hell did my life turn out like this?" he mumbled to himself. He set the bottles down and unslung the Remington from his shoulder. He lay the rifle on the ground and dug out a zippo lighter they'd found underneath the bar. "What am I fucking doing here?"

More terrified screams from the hotel gave Max his answer. It was simple. There were people who needed him. If he survived, he could contemplate the deeper meaning of it all—his motivations and the life choices that led him to this moment. But right now, they needed him. And that's all that mattered.

With a quick flick of the zippo, Max lit the fuse to a bottle of overproof rum. He watched the soaked rag flare up, took two big steps, and launched the bottle overhand.

"Eat that, motherfucker!"

The bottle tumbled out of the moonlit sky and crashed against the midsection of the freak's exoskeleton. Flames flared up from its hard shell, but the monstrous bug barely noticed. It kept burrowing into the hotel, searching for prey. Max swore he heard its mandibles gnashing.

He lit another bottle and tossed it with a grunt. This one shattered closer to the freak's head. Flames spread across its body, spewing black smoke. But the creature still didn't react. It was like using a cigarette lighter on a tank. The thing's armor was just too damn thick.

Max stood there, feeling powerless and small. Then he recalled the moment at the bungalows when Erin cut open the other freak's belly… *Its soft underbelly.*

Quickly, he flicked the zippo to life again and lit the last booze bomb, a 50/50 mix of Sambuca and lighter fluid. The fuse flared bright. Max held his breath a moment then tossed it underhand, like he was throwing a bowling ball. The bottle skipped along the manicured lawn. It bounced twice, rolled beneath the creature's massive body, and…

Nothing. The bottle didn't shatter.

Goddamn it! Max exhaled and felt his shoulders stoop. There was one chance left. He scooped the rifle off the ground and took aim. There was plenty of moonlight, but Max could barely spot the bottle's glowing fuse beneath the insect's hulking shadow.

Last bullet, he reminded himself. Then he squeezed the trigger.

The Remington kicked. The bottle exploded. Leaping flames engulfed the freak's underside. It convulsed, slashing its tail and whipping its segmented body around and around. A terrible hiss echoed across the resort grounds. Rationally, Max knew the creature's scurrying legs caused the noise. But right then, he would've sworn it sounded like the dying blonde's anguished cry.

The ex-marine grunted out a cheer and pumped his fist in the air. His celebration died instantly. Flames rising from its body, the massive centipede whirled to face Max's direction. A cluster of cold black eyes stared down at him with prehistoric malevolence.

Max backpedaled one… two… three steps. Then he spun and ran for his life.

TWENTY-THREE

Moonlight glistened off the surging ocean. Alexander's fishing boat churned through the waters nearly a kilometer from Paradise Island's north shore. The Frenchman never looked back. He piloted the fishing boat over the crest of one rolling wave. Then another. The boat rocked in its wake, sending something behind him clattering against the deck.

Merde!

Alexander suspected the source of the clatter was a falling jar—the same jar that once held pickled pigs' feet but now housed a very special specimen. He imagined the glass shattering and the little freak escaping. That fucking thing loose on the boat? No, that would not do at all.

Without hesitation, the Frenchman cut the engines and stumbled back to the deck. Water sloshed across the boards of the swaying boat, and Alexander's suede shoes slipped out from under him. He fell face first, flopping hard against the deck like the shark he had hauled in just that morning. Alexander lay there a moment, trying to catch his breath, tasting dirty salt water on his lips. A groan escaped his lips, and he was about to spit another curse. But then Alexander turned his head and the words died in his throat.

He was eye-to-eye with a mutant centipede.

Thankfully, the glass had held. The freak was still trapped within the jar. The Frenchman let out a relieved sigh and got to his feet. Finding his balance, he lifted the jar from the deck to inspect it in the moonlight.

Inside, 100 legs scratched furiously against the glass, trying to find purchase. The creature's rattling hiss sent vibrations through the jar. To Alexander, the hiss sounded full of torment and desperation, which made the Frenchman smile.

Another wave slapped the boat's hull and Alexander's smile vanished. He slipped and fell again, and the jar fumbled out of his grasp, shattering against the deck. The impact sent the centipede tumbling towards the stern. It came to rest in a dark corner among a tangle of ropes and gear.

No! No! No!

Heart racing, Alexander whirled around and scampered towards the pilothouse. There was no time to get to his feet, so he kept on his hands and knees, sloshing along the wet deck. If he could just get inside and slam the door shut. If he could just…

Alexander howled. Mandibles as sharp as barbecue forks stabbed through his pant leg into his calf. Frantically, he kicked and thrashed, trying to dislodge the little fuck, but the creature had latched on tightly. A moment later, pain gave way to numbness. An iciness took hold of his leg, sending a cold wave traveling up his veins towards his groin.

A single word screamed inside Alexander's skull. *Venom!*

"Gaaah!" He grit his teeth together and yanked hard on the insect freak. Once…. twice… three times…

Finally, the freak came free. Alexander felt a loose chunk of calf meat roll down his pant leg followed by a warm surge of blood that soaked through the fabric. The centipede squirmed in the Frenchman's grip, mandibles gnashing for his face.

"No, you little bastard." Alexander tried shuffling back towards the pilothouse, but the venom caused his leg to go dead. He lost his footing, toppled forward, and fell overboard with a splash.

The dark sea swallowed him. Alexander desperately clawed at the water, trying to fight his way up towards the shimmering moonlight. He gulped down a mouthful of salt water and his chest went tight. Alexander had always been an excellent swimmer, having been taught as a child by the finest coaches in France. None of that mattered now. He couldn't kick with his right leg, since it was full of centipede venom. So Alexander relied on his left and paddled hard with his hands.

He broke the surface and took in a deep, hacking breath of sea air. Bobbing there in the moonlight, it took him a full minute to remember the centipede.

Panic overtook him and the Frenchman thrashed around in circles, searching the dark water for the little beast. He had been lucky with the first bite. It had been quick, and the creature had not been able to inject much venom into his blood stream. But if that thing bit him again, there was no way Alexander could make it back to the boat. The poison would seize his muscles in its icy grip and the sea would claim him.

Moments later, Alexander spotted the little freak being carried off in the opposite direction by a wave. The Frenchman breathed easy and even felt a smile tug at his lips. He was going to make it. All he had to do was swim back to the boat, and he would be free.

He began swimming, watching the vessel a few meters away rising and falling on undulating waves. Alexander was not concerned. Even hampered by his leg, the Frenchman was sure he could reach it.

A splash to his left caught Alexander's attention. A slice of dark movement swam underneath the moonlit sea. A blade of cartilage and flesh broke the surface and cut through the water, carving out a circular path around the Frenchman.

His heart stopped and he found himself treading water rather than propelling forward. The shark narrowed its path. Then the fin vanished.

Fear overtook Alexander and he kicked hard towards the drifting boat. He did not get far before another fin appeared. Then another. Alexander remembered his wounded calf and his pantleg soaked with gore.

Blood in the water, he thought right before the first bite came.

Alexander thrashed. The surging waterline drowned out his shrieks of pain, reducing them to garbled gags. He felt his own blood pool around him, turning warm water even warmer.

A moment later, all three tiger sharks were on him.

***

Max ran like the prey he was. His arms pumped. His shoes dug into the lawn. Sweat streamed down his brow, and his breath became short and ragged. He didn't dare look back. Max was sure the freak was right behind him. He felt the heat of its smoldering armored hide. He smelled its burning carapace, a revolting acidic, alien stench. He heard its angry hiss, a sound that rattled his skull and drowned out all other noise. One word screamed over and over inside the ex-marine's mind.

Move. Move. Move.

Max felt the soft grass beneath him give way to the hard concrete of the deck. The resort's Olympic-sized pool stretched out before him. Its lights were off, and the moon gleamed across its mirrored surface.

"Get ready," Max yelled. He prayed Erin heard him from her hiding spot. Prayed this would work.

Two more long strides and Max dove in. He swam beneath the dark water for several yards, kicking with every last ounce of his strength. He couldn't see the sides or bottom of the pool. He couldn't see what was in there with him.

The mega freak slithered into the pool the moment Max broke the surface. He didn't know if the creature was chasing him or just trying to extinguish the flames that scorched its belly. Either way, the thing's bulk created a violent wave that scooped Max up and spat him to the other side of the pool.

Max made a mad scramble onto the pool deck and flopped on his back. Finally, he saw the monster. Jesus, it was bigger than he thought. Its long, segmented body stretched nearly the entire length of the pool. Steam rose from its shell, shrilling like an angry tea kettle. The mutant's sharp forelegs punched into the concrete deck and pulled its front segment from the pool. Water dripped like saliva from its terrible, clicking mandibles. All those cold, dark eyes stared at Max with malice.

Max skuttled backwards as a leg speared the ground inches away from him. "Do it!" he screamed, again praying that Erin heard him. "Fucking, do it!"

She did.

Max heard the sharp clack of an electrical breaker being switched. A split-second later, the pool lights snapped on. And so did every piece of electronic equipment they could find—the guitar, bass, amps, keyboard, stage lights, several electric fans, even a fucking bar blender. All of them sat on the bottom of the pool, their cords stretching up out of the water to power strips.

Minutes ago, while Max had crept towards the creature with makeshift bombs, Erin had buzzed around the pool deck in a near panic, getting everything ready.

Now, hundreds of thousands of volts surged through the water. The whole pool hummed and vibrated with electricity. Whisps of smoke replaced the steam rising from the massive centipede's body. It thrashed wildly, a hundred frantic legs slashing at the side of the pool, trying to find purchase. Wild arcs of water sprayed in all directions.

Max crab-walked backwards, shuffling out of a pool-side puddle—getting distance between himself and the thrashing monstrosity. He sensed movement behind him and saw Erin rushing away from an electrical box mounted on a nearby post. The redhead slowed as she approached him, eyes wide with awe.

"Holy shit. It worked."

More smoke rose from the creature as small fires flared to life along the length of its body. The thing quit thrashing and froze in place. Its body vibrated so violently, Max thought its legs might rip right out of their sockets. But the beast forced itself to take one trembling, measured step forward. Then another. Slowly, it pulled its front segment from the water even as its hind segments shuddered and cooked.

Erin backed up, but her eyes never left the monstrosity. "It's... It's getting out."

Desperate, Max scanned the pavilion, looking for a weapon—any weapon. Like a beacon in the night, one called out to him. He rushed to the pavilion and grabbed hold of the tacky Paradise Island sign hanging behind the bar. Neon palm trees and glowing cursive letters forced him to squint as he tugged with both hands.

Behind him, Max could hear Erin's voice, quavering with fear. "Whatever you're doing, do it fast."

Max chomped his teeth together and pulled hard. Screws and anchors ripped out of the wall and the sign wrenched free. With a grunt, Max hefted it and jogged back towards the pool. The sign hummed with electricity. It was long and awkward to carry, but not as heavy as he thought. Max only hoped its extension cord was long enough.

Whipping its antennae back and forth, the creature shook its head wildly. It saw Max approaching and tried to lunge out of the pool to snatch him up. But the volts surging through its body hampered the mutant's speed. Max ducked under its clicking mandibles and heaved the sign into the water.

If someone asked him later, Max would deny it. But right then he swore the expression on the creature's face had somehow changed. Its eyes, once full of predatory menace filled with something else—*fear.*

The second the neon *Paradise Island* sign hit the water, the monstrous bug went all herky-jerky— quivering with electric spasms. Sparks erupted from its joints and flames rose from its shell. The pool light flickered creating a strobe effect, throwing the creature's shuddering shadow across the resort lawn. Steam and smoke poured from its twitching mouth. Then—like the smaller freaks before it—the freak's segments became super-heated pressure cookers. They expanded, bigger and bigger until…

POP! The freak's body burst like an engorged maggot, spurting purple goop in all directions. Finally, its inert skull thudded down to the pool deck while the rest of its body convulsed with the last sparks of life.

For a long time, Max and Erin just stood side-by-side in silence, catching their breath. It didn't matter that most of the monster's guts had been blown across the lawn. Neither of them dared to get any closer. Both had seen enough horror movies to know that was a death sentence. Instead, they gazed at each other until the flickering pool light finally died out. Without a word, Erin sunk into Max's arms, and they held each other up in the darkness.

TWENTY-FOUR

They never got their proper date with the white tablecloths and wine lists. Instead, Max and Erin spent three days and nights together at the Mai Tai Inn in Papeete, a cheap seaside motel worn down by the tropical sun and salt air. After their evacuation from Paradise Island, survivors were ushered to the Mai Tai to recuperate from wounds, both physical and psychological. Max didn't know who footed the bill for the motel or the medical staff that treated them. Maybe the Red Cross or a Tahitian equivalent. Truth was, he didn't really care.

No reporters came to talk to them. No officials. No lawyers. And they saw nothing about the incident online. It was like it never happened.

He and Erin shared a small one-bedroom suite with bamboo shades and flowered wallpaper. There, they ate room service, drank the Inn's signature cocktail, and made sweaty love with the windows open, the night's hot breezes wafting in. But all the rum and sex couldn't stop the darkness from creeping into their dreams. In sleep, Erin clung close to him, wincing and twitching, as if something was chasing her.

"Easy does it, college girl," he'd whisper to her, brushing long red hair from her face. "You're safe now."

But even as he said it, Max eyed the dark corners of the room, unconsciously listening for hissing.

There was no talk of their future together. They took everything day by day, and often found themselves on the beach under the mid-morning sun, just watching boats coast across crystal blue waters. That's where they were on the fourth day when the helicopter came.

Max spotted it first, a UH-1N Iroquois breaking through a cloud bank, a dark dragonfly against blue skies. Affectionately given the name Huey, it was an ancient chopper, but still in service with armed forces. This one, however, was painted matte black with no insignias.

Yeah, that's not suspicious. Not at all.

Max shaded his eyes and watched the craft whip its way towards them from the sea. Erin caught him looking and slipped on a cheap pair of sunglasses so she could watch too.

"How much you wanna bet they're here for us," she said.

"No deal."

The Huey came down a hundred feet away, its blades kicking up a torrent of sand and sending rippling waves to fight against the tide. Max shielded his eyes from the blowing sand but didn't get up. They'd send someone for him in time.

And they did—a handsome, broad-shouldered African American guy in his early thirties. He wore jeans and a polo-shirt instead of a uniform, but Max knew right away he was military by the way he carried himself.

"Sergeant McTavish?"

"Not for a long time." Max let his gaze wander back to the ocean while Erin looked up at the guy, her fierce eyes unwavering.

"But you are Maxwell McTavish." It wasn't a question.

"You already know that or you wouldn't be here."

"There's someone who would like a word with you, sir." The guy gestured to the chopper.

"This somebody got a name?"

"He's got a rank," said the man. "And it's colonel."

"Guess I'm up for a chat." Max took his time standing up and brushed the sand from the seat of his shorts. Erin stood next to him. She wore a tank top with bikini bottoms and a touristy, *Mai Tai Inn* baseball cap to protect her pale cheeks from the sun.

"I'm a little underdressed for a colonel," Erin said, straightening her cap. "Think he'll mind?"

"I'm sorry, Miss Johannson," the guy said, not looking sorry at all. "Just Mr. McTavish."

"Where I go, she goes," said Max, and before the military dude could object, the two of them trudged across the beach towards the helicopter, side-by-side.

A few tourists and locals had gathered, but none of them got close to the Huey—maybe sensing it was a harbinger of trouble. Max hoped they were wrong.

The blades had stopped their spin and the dust had settled. The hull door was open and Max saw the man in its cabin, tall with short-cropped white hair. He was sixty-something but fit, in a black button up shirt and cargo pants. He had a pair of aviator sunglasses propped up on his head so he could squint down at an iPad.

"How's it going, Colonel?" Max asked.

The older man took a few moments to finish what he was reading before looking up. "I hear you're a monster hunter now?"

"Christ, how did you find out so fast?"

The colonel slipped his aviators down to hide his eyes. He swung out of the cabin but didn't offer to shake hands. Neither did Max. "I've got my ways," said the colonel. "And four days isn't so fast. Is it all true?"

Erin glanced at Max. It looked like she was crinkling her eyebrows, confused by the whole situation, but Max couldn't be sure with her sunglasses and cap. "What's going on?" she asked. "You act like you know each other."

Max shrugged then waved his hand with an exaggerated flourish. "Allow me to introduce Colonel Howard McTavish. My father."

Now she really was crinkling those eyebrows. "Wait. What?"

"We'll dispense with the pleasantries onboard the chopper," said McTavish. He was already climbing back inside the Huey's cabin. "Got a destroyer waiting for us out there."

Max let out a frustrated chuckle. *Nothing ever changes.* "No, Dad," he said. "We're not going anywhere with you. Not until you tell us what this is about."

Slowly, the older McTavish slid off his aviators and fixed his son with a dead-serious gaze. "I'll make it simple for you. Your country needs you, son."

"Needs me?" Max shook his head, dumbfounded. "What could it possibly need me for?"

"Killing monsters," said the colonel.

THE END?

Mike MacLean is responsible for writing the most outrageous monster movies ever to prowl cable TV, including *Sharktopus*, *Piranhaconda*, and *Dinocroc vs. Supergator*, all produced by Hollywood legend Roger Corman. Mike then leapt into the Hellish world of *Lady Death*, co-writing the incredibly successful Coffin Comics line of graphic novels with independent icon Brian Pulido. Mike's other credits include a sci-fi kaiju thriller and a slew of bone-breaking crime stories that bloodied the pages of *The Best American Mystery Stories* and *Ellery Queen Mystery Magazine*.

SEVEREDPRESS

Check out other great

Cryptid Novels!

J.H. Moncrieff

RETURN TO DYATLOV PASS

In 1959, nine Russian students set off on a skiing expedition in the Ural Mountains. Their mutilated bodies were discovered weeks later. Their bizarre and unexplained deaths are one of the most enduring true mysteries of our time. Nearly sixty years later, podcast host Nat McPherson ventures into the same mountains with her team, determined to finally solve the mystery of the Dyatlov Pass incident. Her plans are thwarted on the first night, when two trackers from her group are brutally slaughtered. The team's guide, a superstitious man from a neighboring village, blames the killings on yetis, but no one believes him. As members of Nat's team die one by one, she must figure out if there's a murderer in their midst—or something even worse—before history repeats itself and her group becomes another casualty of the infamous Dead Mountain.

Gerry Griffiths

CRYPTID ZOO

As a child, rare and unusual animals, especially cryptid creatures, always fascinated Carter Wilde. Now that he's an eccentric billionaire and runs the largest conglomerate of high-tech companies all over the world, he can finally achieve his wildest dream of building the most incredible theme park ever conceived on the planet... CRYPTID ZOO. Even though there have been apparent problems with the project, Wilde still decides to send some of his marketing employees and their families on a forced vacation to assess the theme park in preparation for Opening Day. Nick Wells and his family are some of those chosen and are about to embark on what will become the most terror-filled weekend of their lives—praying they survive. STEP RIGHT UP AND GET YOUR FREE PASS... TO CRYPTID ZOO

SEVEREDPRESS

@severedpress
f /severedpress

Check out other great

Cryptid Novels!

P.K. Hawkins

THE CRYPTID FILES

Fresh out of the academy with top marks, Agent Bradley Tennyson is expecting to have the pick of cases and investigations throughout the country. So he's shocked when instead he is assigned as the new partner to "The Crag," an agent well past his prime. He thinks the assignment is a punishment. It's anything but.Agent George Crag has been doing this job for far longer than most, and he knows what skeletons his bosses have in the closet and where the bodies are buried. He has pretty much free reign to pick his cases, and he knows exactly which one he wants to use to break in his new young partner: the disappearance and murder of a couple of college kids in a remote mountain town.Tennyson doesn't realize it, but Crag is about to introduce him to a world he never believed existed: The Cryptid Files, a world of strange monsters roaming in the night. Because these murders have been going on for a long time, and evidence is mounting that the murderer may just in fact be the legendary Bigfoot.

Gerry Griffiths

DOWN FROM BEAST MOUNTAIN

A beast with a grudge has come down from the mountain to terrorize the townsfolk of Porterville. The once sleepy town is suddenly wide awake. Sheriff Abel McGuire and game warden Grant Tanner frantically investigate one brutal slaying after another as they follow the blood trail they hope will eventually lead to the monstrous killer. But they better hurry and stop the carnage before the census taker has to come out and change the population sign on the edge of town to ZERO.

SEVEREDPRESS

@severedpress
/severedpress

Check out other great

Cryptid Novels!

Hunter Shea
LOCH NESS REVENGE

Deep in the murky waters of Loch Ness, the creature known as Nessie has returned. Twins Natalie and Austin McQueen watched in horror as their parents were devoured by the world's most infamous lake monster. Two decades later, it's their turn to hunt the legend. But what lurks in the Loch is not what they expected. Nessie is devouring everything in and around the Loch, and it's not alone. Hell has come to the Scottish Highlands. In a fierce battle between man and monster, the world may never be the same. Praise for THEY RISE : "Outrageous, balls to the wall...made me yearn for 3D glasses and a tub of popcorn, extra butter!" – The Eyes of Madness "A fast-paced, gore-heavy splatter fest of sharksploitation." The Werd "A rocket paced horror story. I enjoyed the hell out of this book." Shotgun Logic Reviews

C.G. Mosley
BAKER COUNTY BIGFOOT CHRONICLE

Marie Bledsoe only wants her missing brother Kurt back. She'll stop at nothing to make it happen and, with the help of Kurt's friend Tony, along with Sheriff Ray Cochran, Marie embarks on a terrifying journey deep into the belly of the mysterious Walker Laboratory to find him. However, what she and her companions find lurking in the laboratory basement is beyond comprehension. There are cryptids from the forest being held captive there and something...else. Enjoy this suspenseful tale from the mind of C.G. Mosley, author of Wood Ape. Welcome back to Baker County, a place where monsters do lurk in the night!

Printed in Great Britain
by Amazon

63037087R00087